Twinkletoes

A Tale of Limehouse

By

Thomas Burke

Author of "Limehouse Nights," "London Lamps," etc.

NEW YORK
ROBERT M. McBRIDE & COMPANY
1918

Published 1918

To

Cranstoun Metcalfe

.

I

MONICA MINASI was named Twinkletoes by the teacher at the Council
School which she attended in her
early years; and you had but to glance at
her tempestuous limbs to realize that no
other name belonged to her.

When she arrived in Shantung Place,
Poplar, she had a mother and a father. But
within a week she had other friends. Mother
at first didn't like her to play in the streets
as other children did. She said it would
make her grow up rough, and run in the
gutters, and tear her clothes; and that nobody respected a mother who allowed her
children to run in the gutters. But there
were nice differences in Shantung Place; it
was easy to find a sympathetic set; and
when Twinkletoes told her mother how nicely
the Matchkey boys and girls behaved, she
was allowed to play in the street after school,
so long as she didn't run in the gutter, and
came in before dark.

7

Twinkletoes

You see, Twinkletoes hadn't got a garden, because she and Mum and Dad lived in one room. Dad worked all day as a sign-writer, but only Twinkletoes seemed to recognize what a wonderful sign-writer he was, because, however hard he worked, he never got much money. And he wanted money; he often told Mum so; not for himself, but in order to give Twinkletoes a good show; for, as he often said, "If a kid—girl especially—don't get a good send-off these days, she don't never get nowhere."

Still Twinkletoes was happy. Living in one room does not necessarily imply living in a piggery, a miserable corner of a miserable garret, all dirt and disorder. It all depends on the manager. Mum knew all the tricks. That one room was not a piggery; no, a snuggery. For a long time Twinkletoes thought it diplomatic to hide the horrid truth, fearing, from what she had overheard between Mum and Dad, that it carried some kind of social outlawry. But

8

she let it out gradually to the Matchkey boys and girls, and when Mum said they might come to tea, and when they said they didn't care whether it was one room or Windsor Castle, Twinkletoes touched heaven.

The elder Matchkey boy adored her. Her peach-soft face; her nineteen golden curls; her eyes like flowers that made a resting-place for a thousand expressive butterflies; her epigrammatic legs in their darned stockings; her black silk coat and the flaming vermilion tam-o'-shanter and the glory that dances about a girl when she is twelve; all thrilled the Matchkey boy as he waited at the gate of the boys' playground at the Council School to see her turn the corner.

At dinner-time they would walk home together, turning down side streets to see if Twinkletoes' Dad was working; and when they saw a brown ladder outside a shop they knew that Dad was atop of it, with his palette and his knife and his brush, creating wonderful golden words, like:

> THE HOPE AND ANCHOR
> FREE HOUSE

or

> THE KING'S HEAD
> CHARRINGTON & CO'S ENTIRE

or

> GOOD PULL UP FOR CARMEN
> NO CONNECTION WITH THE HOUSE OPPOSITE

And Dad, a little wiry elflike man, would look down at them, and spit, very carefully out of their way, and say:

"Well, old Cockalorum, 'ow's she going?"

And Twinkletoes would look up, and say:

"Ain't my Dad wonderful? Ain't he the cleverest man in the world?"

At one o'clock Dad would descend, wipe his hands on the seat of his trousers, and breathe, "Ah!" heavily. "Some day," he would say, "we're going to make money. Young Twinks here 'as got to 'ave a piano,

some'ow. She's got a knack for it. Trouble
about one room is, you can't get a piano in,
even if you can afford one. She 'as to go
round to Auntie Alice's to practice now.
But, never mind, we'll wangle it 'fore long.
We'll 'ave a piano, *and* a room to put it in,
not 'alf we won't. Come on, shavers!"

"Ain't my Dad wonderful?"

The Matchkey children agreed that he
was, chiefly because, producing little else
of value, he had yet produced Twinkletoes,
his "old Cockalorum." It was Twinkletoes
who had played pianoforte solos at the
breaking-up entertainment at the Council
School, when the more socially comfortable
Matchkeys had listened to glittering pieces
of Italian opera, which, to her, were the
loveliest music in the world. They were
amazed and faint with adoration as they
watched those tiny hands fetching clusters
of colored unnameable dreams from that
magic thing which was a piano. Other
children, too, of the Poplar district, were

11

on that night as the shepherds when the heavenly hosts brought to them a message.

"Ain't she a dam queer kid?" chuckled Dad Minasi to the elder Matchkey. "She's going to be something 'fore she finishes, I know. T'other day, f'rinstance, she come running in—I was shaving meself at the time, at the table, and nearly cut meself— I didn't 'alf swear—and out she comes with: 'Dad, I've found out 'ow people 'ave babies!' Think of it—a kid like 'er. I don't suppose you know that—eh?" The Matchkey boy blushed, and looked awfully surprised. "But I soon shut her up. 'Well,' I says, 'if you 'ave, you needn't do a song and dance about it. You aint the only one that knows!' I says. Just like that. Soon shut 'er up. But she's a fair corker, she is. All the time. She'll be something 'ot when she's a bit older, I give yeh *my* word! Only," he said impressively to Matchkey, who gravely responded to the confidence, "what you want nowadays is Influence. Influence. Or Money. Can't

12

do nothing without one or other of 'em. Otherwise yeh don't get a chance, sonny. I might 'a' been something if I'd 'ad Influence. Or Money. Well, I can't get no influence nowhere, so I've got to get money. Give 'er 'er chance, like. See? She'll be something, you take it from me. Can't tell yeh what. And I don't care much, s'long's she's 'appy. . . . Coming along to tea to-morrow, ain't yeh? Good. You'll 'ave to take pot-luck, y'know. Can't do things in much of a lah-di-dah way in one room, y'know. But any friends of Twinks is welcome. Toodle-oo, sonny."

Living in one room is a preparation for all the highest comforts and deepest struggles of life. Only a genius can make happiness from such rough stuff. And Mum, aided and abetted by Twinkletoes, created happiness for the three of them. They were happy in the heroic makeshifts that were imperative, and in the gentle content that grew up around them like the nasturtiums that grew in the box on the window-sill under Twinkletoes' careful hands. The nasturtiums flourished because there was the sunshine of Shantung Place to warm them and the water which Twinkletoes carried up two flights of stairs to refresh them. Domestic happiness flourished likewise.

Mum allowed the company to make toast for Twinkletoes' first tea-party, and the guests sat round the fire with their hostess, and told their little life-stories and their ambitions. One desired to be a bank manager, because it was nice, clean work. One said he would paint pictures, and the company yelled derisively. Somebody wanted to do something with engines. But when Twinkletoes was asked what she was going to be she replied patly and firmly: "Going to be a dancer."

Nobody laughed; for even the children felt that the fairies had decided for her. A star must have danced when she was born.

They sat staring into the fire after tea,

14

and as they stared into the glowing, hissing mass (for Twinkletoes, with unchallengeable aplomb, had picked up and carried home some wood blocks from East India Dock Road, where repairs were proceeding), they dreamed their separate dreams. Wonderful visions were given them.

They saw bright roads along which they should travel. They saw great enterprises and successes, and the external trappings that, to the minds of Shantung Place, spelt glory. They all wanted to get on. They wanted to have houses of their own and a garden. They wanted clean collars every day. They wanted to go out to "late dinner," as "gentlefolks" in the West did. They wanted to go to theatres—oh, theatres every night for Twinkletoes—and to book their seats instead of waiting outside gallery doors, as they did once a year for the local pantomime at the Quayside. The boys were going to have silk hats and white waistcoats and frock coats for Sundays, and the girls

15

were going to have all the silken frillies that
"ladies' children" had; and if they got on
wonderfully well they might ride in hansom
cabs sometimes; perhaps they could even
keep a servant.

All those things they saw, and some of the
company have attained their desire. But
they did not see, and it was a kindly veil that
hid from them, the road that Twinkletoes
was to travel.

In those days they were too young properly to know her. She was gracefully old
beyond her years. Angel and elf she was,
and human, too; so human that she gave to
all things and to all men love, after the
ecstatic worship reserved for Dad. She
never grumbled when times were bad. She
laughed when there was no coal in the
scuttle; she chirruped when there was no
Sunday dinner; and sat instead on Dad's
knee, and made him talk of his forlorn past.
She forgave all offences, and brought divine
merriment to those one-room feastings and

escapades. She found everything good, and her motto for all seasons and occasions, gurgled deliciously, with not very clean hands clasped to a pinafored bosom, was:

"Ooh! Ain't people and things *Lovely!*"

But those days passed, and with them her circle of friends. Parents "got on," and moved from Poplar to stately suburbs, taking the youngsters and the secret glory that should never be recaptured.

When Twinkletoes was twelve, and the Matchkey circle was broken into bits that scattered themselves along North and South London, Mum died. Dad, in a now-or-never mood, mysteriously and decisively threw up the sign-writing and started a die-stamping business, and money began to reach the Minasi household. They moved from one room to a small cottage. Twinkletoes received long courses in music and dancing, and at fifteen she was leader of a local juvenile dancing troupe, and had forgotten the comrades of her early days. She was a woman now, and had begun to make new friends.

Dad had kept his word. They had got that piano, and the room to put it in. Twinkletoes had had her chance, had taken it, and, in a small way, had arrived.

"Can't think where she gets it all from," Dad would say, when discussing her success with his friends. "Every time I look at 'er I feel fair knocked over—flabbergasted, like—to think that I did it. Or me and the missus between us. Never thought, that night, that I'd get a kid like this. Wonder 'ow we did it? Must 'ave gorn upstairs backwards, or something."

II

IN CHINATOWN lurks the Blue Lantern, a tavern that was once the haunt of good and gay Bohemians, but is now only used by artists and poets seeking atmosphere.

On a grey evening between seasons, in its grand days, Chuck Lightfoot, ex-manager to Battling Burrows, the Poplar Terror, cuddled the counter of its four-ale bar and discoursed to his companion, Hank Hogan, on certain things good to be known concerning life and its mysteries. Chuck was haunted by a grief, and was trying vainly to drown it. Gin and coke and chandoo may bless many a bruise, and wipe out many a stain upon the heart of man, but there are some wounds which neither material drugs nor the balm of time can heal. Many beers cannot quench them; neither can the white stuff drown them. Chuck had worked over his with beer, li-un, whisky and powder; yet was it as lively as ever. It throbbed and burned. It racked him. It bled.

19

All Poplar knew of his grief, and fellows in the bar would nod and nudge and say: "Old Chuck's on it again. Silly devil. 'E'll get what's comin' to 'im, right enough."

The trouble was first marked when he ceased to call at the Galloping Horses for a half-pint, of an evening, and took to lounging in the Blue Lantern, swigging pints of the Old.

This evening he put down six in as many minutes; then smashed his pewter on the bar and called for more.

"Enough to make a chap go on the bat," he explained to Hank, "what I bin through the last month or two . . ."

"Ar," said Hank, a little fellow with a deprecating manner and a deceptive face of bovine stupidity crowned with explosive red hair.

"I should say so." And Chuck took his tankard, and gulped largely, as though swallowing something more potent and substantial than the Lantern's Old.

20

"I bin in 'ell," he stated, in a voice that succeeded in being anguished without being absurd. " 'Ell. Nothing less."

"Ar," said Hank.

The lights of Chinatown across the way stammered through the dusk. Songs and smokes curled from the Quarter. Strange kisses and embraces hung on every breath of air, and in that evening hour pale arms seemed to invite to remote, forbidden beauties. Against these forces, the frankly lighted electric cars, tearing towards Aldgate, joined in level combat.

Chuck finished his eighth, let the dregs slip slackly to the floor, and shook a hammer-like arm at nothing. "Christ almighty! Blast everything."

"Oh, I dunno," said Hank, between swigs. "Why everything? Seems to me . . ."

"What th'ell d'you know about it?"

"Well, I thought . . ."

"Huh." Chuck flung away from him and came swiftly back. He spread disdainful hands. He tapped Hank on the chest. "What'd you say 'f you 'eard of a chap of twenty-nine in love with a girl of fourteen?"

"I'd say same as everyone. I'd say it was all blasted rot. I'd say 'e was barmy. Or a dirty beast. Orf 'is rocker. Nobody else'd wanter love a kid."

"Oh." Chuck sucked a Woodbine. "That's what *you* think. I thought it's what you *would* think," he said, after lifting and setting down an empty pewter. "Shows 'ow blasted much you know about it. Why can't a man fall in love with a girl in short frocks and still be all right? Tell me that, old son. Why can't 'e? Eh?"

"Why, because 'e . . ." Hank sought for explanations. In his plain mind the answer was fairly obvious; yet when he came to make it he realised that it could not be made. He was right, he knew. But what was the reason? "Why, 'cos 'e . . . 'cos she . . . I mean, anyone can see that it ain't—that 'e can't. There ain't nothing in

22

it. Course 'e wouldn't," he jerked, in the futile anger of a man who is asked to prove conclusively that white is white.

"Well, yer wrong," said Chuck huskily. "Am I barmy?"

"Not yet. But yeh will be if yeh keep this 'ere game up much longer." He patted the bar with a hairy hand, and his moist eyes became moister with affection. "I'm old enough to be yer father, Chuck. Why don't yeh drink steady, like me? You 'ad a good job what you lorst through this, and I dunno what'll be the end of yeh. I've 'ad my time. This 'ere bar's my waitin'-room, like. But you, lad—fer Christ's sake pull yesself together."

"No good. If you'd bin through what I'm going through . . ."

"I 'ave, old sport, and I'm still 'ere."

"I ain't barmy, and I ain't a beast. But I love old Minasi's kid—like I dunno what. For the last two years. Never loved anything like this before. Fifteen, she is now

23

—nearly sixteen—and me—I'm twenty-nine. And married. But I'd die if I could save that kid the least bit of pain or—do anything she wanted done, like. 'Elp 'er in any way. Absolutely."

Hank stared, convinced that Chuck was very drunk, yet feeling the truth was coming out of the tankard. Chuck caught the look.

"Oh, I know. I know it's all—kind o' wrong. And yet—oh, I know." He waved inarticulate arms. "Yeh can't tell me nothing about the pleading business that I ain't already thought of. I love young Twinkletoes. There's an end of it. And I can't eat or sleep or do anything. Old bloke—I've woke up in the night, and found meself blubbing." He folded his arms, leant to the bar, and examined his brown-booted feet. "Oh, Christ!" he snapped, in such a voice that old Dickery-Dock, the landlord, looked across in some concern.

"I love 'er. 'Ow she goes about the streets every day and everybody don't fall in love with 'er I dunno. 'Ank—'ave you seen that little black frock she wears, and the way it crumples up? 'Ave you seen those yellow curls of 'ers? And 'er little brown shoes and stockings? And the way she smiles at yeh? You've seen 'er dance, ain't you, at the Quayside? . . . Gaw. If we could only get away somewhere—just for an hour or two —so's I could be near 'er, alone, and talk to 'er. I don't want to touch 'er. She's too— kind of 'oly. You ain't ever loved no one. Else you'd know. Not proper."

"Oh. Ain't I?"

"But I can't even take 'er for a tram ride. People 'd talk. Blast their dirty minds. . . . Oh, of course, it's all out o' joint. Nobody'd understand 'ow I can 'ear 'er voice all day long through everything, and 'ow every- where I look I see 'er face. On the floor; on the wall; in the sky; even in the bottom of this bloody, dirty tankard. Gimme another, Dickery. She comes to the Works nearly every day, and if she stands near me, or 'er

25

frock touches me, I feel, when she's gorn, like as though she'd wrenched me arm or me ear orf. What'm I going to do?"

"You bett' go away," said Hank, in the level tones of one perfunctorily offering advice, which he knows will not be accepted. "Bett' go away. Knock orf this jag game, and git orf to the Forest, and go in training for a bit. Out at Chingford or Lambourn End. Get the Duke to go wi' yeh, and do some stiff work on the ball."

"Huh. If this is love, Gawd 'elp anyone in love. I 'ang round 'er 'ouse sometimes, though it 'urts like 'ell. . . . Oh, what's it bin and 'appened to me for? Why me? . . . Drink up and 'ave another. Dickery!"

"Yer in a rotten state," said Hank; "but there y'are—that's always the way." He drank up and had another, and as his little eyes hovered over the rim of his mug he remarked: "Ar. Talk of the devil. There goes the kid over t'other side. Just caught 'er out the corner o' me eye."

Chuck shot his drink to the counter, tip-toed, and peered over the ground-glass portion of the Lantern's window. Sailing towards Chinatown was a child as lovely and as insolently happy as a lyric. Torrents of bright curls foamed about her shoulders, and the black silk frock clung to her young beauty as though it loved her. The mirror-like candour of her face, undimmed by any breath of the world's abominations, reflected nothing but the serene joy of the moment. Remote seemed her glory from that mephitic chaos. Timid as a wraith that may melt at a touch, she seemed too fragile even for childhood; and the mind shrank from the thought that the deflowering hand of man should rest upon this phantom of a dream.

As Chuck watched her the light of love-madness was in his eyes, and a tense pain was about his lips. He made noises when he noted the glances which the Asiatics turned upon this filigree toy, and the innocently flirtatious smiles with which she responded.

27

More tender of soul than most men, he dared not dream of possessing her; of lacing arms about her; of pressing lip to lip; though every fibre of his being ached for her.

His eyes fell upon the soft fruit of her face. He strained his ears to catch the sound of her crystal voice, and when he heard her cry, "Suffering Jesus!" as she narrowly escaped falling over a cat, he longed to answer it. When she disappeared into the Causeway his hands dropped; he turned away his head, snatched angrily at his mug and drank and drank.

" 'Ere, 'alf a mo," said Hank suddenly, when a double gin followed the last tankard. "Put the brake on, lad. I ain't a-arguing with yeh; I'm a-telling of yeh!"

Chuck spluttered wild oaths. The physical nausea that accompanies great grief had gripped him. His fingers clutched nothing. The reek of the sawdust bar swam about his nose. The lights swam about his eyes in conflict with the half-gloom of the streets.

28

He stared solemnly at Hank, and noted, without wonder, that Hank was leaping grotesquely from floor to ceiling.

"Why can't yeh keep still?" he shouted. Dickery Dock came forward.

"Push 'im 'ome, 'Ank," he said considerately. " 'E's got a skate on."

"That's me. Alwis comes on me, don't it? Reckon I seen every one of the boys 'ome one time or another. Eh?"

"I dessay. Wonderful what you could give away, 'f yeh started talking, 'Ank. Winter sports—seeing the Lantern boys 'ome." He made a snort which served for a chuckle. "Ought to write in the papers, 'Ank. Remensensees of the Blue Lantern. By 'Ank." He exploded. "Shove on, sporty. Get 'im away. 'Ere—'ave one on me—a quick one."

Hank set Chuck on a wooden bench, swallowed the quick one, looped an arm in the lad's and dragged him through the swinging door.

29

The swift air from the river smote Chuck's damp face. "I'm awri'. I'll go 'long 'ome, now. Don' you bother." He braced himself, and set his feet widely apart. The Lascars, parading the streets with their customary, pathetic air of being lost, glanced curiously at him. He threw Hank's arm away. "Christawmighty," he sobbed. "When's it going to end?"

Hank turned about with a platitude on his lips. But Chuck was gone.

Mrs. Lightfoot, to whose quick ears these things had come, had passed her thirtieth year, and, like all women of the district, at that age was old and haggard. She was a large, blonde woman, thin lipped. She had long arms, with cruel, cold hands, and honey-colored hair. Neglected by the well-knit Chuck, she began to be angry before she was sorrowful. She shut herself up at home in bed with halfpenny novelettes and strong tea, and ruminated, while Chuck she knew was going his evil ways and assuaging the eternal grief of things at the Blue Lantern. Once a sweet and mild fellow, as so many pugilists are, he had become, under his sorrow, vindictive; and Cissie knew it.

It was Cissie who leaned from the window of their cottage and witnessed his blasphemous search for his home.

"Blast 'im. Boozing up over that kid, I s'pose. Curse the filthy little wretch. Damn silly to be jealous of a kid, but . . . Oh, I'll fix her some time. I'll fix her."

She heard his fumbling feet on the stair. Then his face, now gone flaccid, popped round the doorway.

"Well, boozey? Seen yer baby sweetheart?" she cried cruelly.

"Levant—you. Find a street and take a walk."

"Pitty ickle sing," she sang. "Rock-a-bye-baby—on the . . ."

" 'Nough o' that. Else I'll mark yeh."

"You do, me lad. It won't pay yeh."

31

"Cut it. Ain't I 'ad enough 'ell, trying to keep straight through this business 'cos o' you, without 'aving to put up with your cackle? Stifle it. Else lay an egg an' done with it." He stood over her, grotesquely furious.

" 'Ow d'you talk to yer baby? Wassums darly-warly going bye-bye all aloney? I s'pose you'd like to go . . ."

Chuck lurched from the wall, grabbed a glass from the table and flung it. It struck Cissie on the mouth. Blood appeared on her lips. She stood up, swaying in the crowding glooms. She laughed in spasms, without mirth. Chuck moved towards her, his face brutalised, his body tense. She laughed again.

"Don't like my cackle, don't yeh? Rather I laid an egg? You look out, me lad." Her voice cracked. Nose and chin were joined by uncomely lines. Her hair tumbled. "Else I may lay an egg," she screamed, "that'll make you look silly!"

32

He lurched nearer, but she seized the poker with swift hands and poised it.

For a few minutes they waited watchfully. Then Chuck made ungainly movements, and found the door. "What a life! Gawd, what a life!" He slithered across the passage to his room. Cissie helped herself to beer, noisily, from a jug.

III

TWINKLETOES, the pocket Venus, the little comrade of all Poplar, flitted, in a cloud of lace and yellow hair, from West India Dock Road to Penny-fields. Her clothes had that touch of disorderly smartness which belongs to the clothes of stage children. So lightly did she move that her feet seemed to kiss the pavements, those pavements she had loved ever since she had walked.

The evening noise of Chinatown was on the air; its acrid tang bit nose and lips. A goods train from the Docks crawled wearily across the Arches. From the river came a voice giving an indecent chantey to a rush of chains and pulley-ropes. Sirens screamed. In a seamen's home faint fingers plucked a melancholy guitar. The brightest and best of the monkeys of the evening paraded the solemn road, brushing shoulders with cat-like Hindoos, jungle-footed Dyaks, and nondescript vagabonds from the Pacific wastes.

34

The black men looked at none of the women; they scanned appreciatively every lovely child whose white-socked legs flittered through the blue twilight.

By day or by dark these streets are scarcely such as one would build one's dreams upon. By day, the impudent sunshine falls upon them, stripping them of their secrets. By night, grey shadows crowd fearfully upon one another. Cold, lean streets turn sharply away, slinking, with malicious eagerness, to nowhere. There are long, faltering streets; brisk, bold streets; mischievous passages and labyrinthine burrows. There are high blocks of houses, apparently inaccessible, showing humane windows across the roofs of others.

But to Twinkletoes all was beautiful. Only once was she jarred, when, as she darted through the alleys, there came off the evening breeze a child's scream, a wail of entreaty, and anomalous noises.

"Suffering Jesus!" she snapped. "Old

Mother Adnitt torturing that kid again. She wants pins stuck in 'er."

She had a low flash-point of temper; was explosively good-natured, explosively combative; and cruelty made her sick. It seemed to her so silly that people should disturb a beautiful world, twisting into wicked shapes the mind that God made so fairly. She knew how beautiful it could be, and she lived to make it more beautiful still. She danced what she saw, and when she saw cruelty she danced that, so that other people might feel as sick as she did, and, she hoped, stop it. People and things were lovely, and Poplar was lovely, and she hated Mrs. Adnitt for spoiling perfection.

Turning into a passage leading from Mandarin Court, she disappeared through a furtive doorway. She was in the Works, the old Dad's Works, the die-stamping business, and her troubles slipped from her. Not once in four years had she missed her daily visit to this little corner of delight. Strangers

36

would have found it dull and squalid and
odorous; but there were half-a-dozen people
in Poplar to whom it was a centre of vibrant
interest. Twinkletoes loved it because it
was Dad's; she had a proprietary as well as
romantic attachment to it. Everything connected with Dad was beautiful. When she
thought of him she thought of all that was
brave and sweet and strong: of Handel's
Largo, or Beethoven's *Fifth Symphony,* or
Schubert's *Songs,* for, as it was through
music that she expressed herself, it was only
to music that she could turn for illustration
of her emotions. Dad had started these
Works, and it was the Works that had provided the means of her education in music
and dancing.

The interest of others had a different basis.
Men would call there during the day and
evening; some splendidly dressed, with just
that over-attention to detail that marked
them from what they desired to be; others,
unclean, in tatters and slops. All entered

casually, with an air of "dropping in," to pass the time of day, though, by tactful stages, they descended with Dad to the basement, and remained sometimes half-an-hour, sometimes two and three hours.

Dad would receive them with his usual chuckle and "Wow-wow, me old Cockalorum," and would speed them on their way with gushes of laughter and timely persiflages. But there were intervals, in the basement, of lively seriousness.

When Twinkletoes entered he was climbing the ladder stair from below. He wore trousers and shirt, with sleeves rolled up. His hands were stained with acid, his expression ruminative. But at the sight of Twinkletoes his face split to a joyous grin.

"Cheerio!" she cried. "Blast these old apples-and-pears of yours—I nearly slipped. Why don't yeh get 'em mended? Well, how's the old pot-and-pan?"

"I'm all right," he answered. "How's the Gawd-forbid?"

38

"Oh, I'm the Big Noise. Same as usual. No complaints. I'm the live wire, I am. Danger on the line for anyone who touches me without rubber gloves. How's biz?"

"Coming in good and plenty. 'Ad yer tea?"

"You bet. And a drop o' Lincoln's Inn with it."

"Marv'lous kid, ain't you," he chuckled, rumpling her cloak of curls.

"Well, Roseleaf said I was slack last night in the Autumn dance. So I thought I'd have a snifter to put me on song and get the juice running properly. . . . Well, boys, how is it?"

The two assistants made non-committal noises.

"Shall I cook for you? Or ain't you through yet?"

"Oh, we're through. Go ahead, Twinks."

"Fair leading 'em on, that's what you are, Twinks," said Dad. "Hiking 'em down the broad and gay white road. Look at 'em

—look at young Perce there—fair wasting away. Look at me—I don't dope, and I could lift 'em both with one hand."

"Chuck it, Dad," said Twinkletoes. "If it amuses 'em, let 'em 'ave it. We were sent here to be happy, and if it makes 'em happy they've a right to it, so long's it don't hurt no one else."

Old Dad Minasi was a man of simple tastes. He liked beer better than wine. He preferred Red Seal to Grand Marnier. He chose to live in Poplar rather than Stamford Hill. He liked shag better than a Cabanas; beef and mutton better than bird; and bread and cheese better than either; and when he took Twinkletoes for a ride on the tram towards the Forest he was as near heaven as he desired to be. With simple food and drink and her society, life was, for him, a bit of all right. And he would chortle mirthfully every hour: "Gawd is love! Hearts are trumps!"

He couldn't understand the dope trick,

40

and he watched with amusement as Twinkletoes danced to a cupboard and produced a
lay out, a lamp, a toey filled with hop, two
pipes, a yen-shi-gow, and a yen-hok. She
lit the lamp and roasted the stuff, delicately
working it until it reached the right con-
sistency. Then she fixed it to the pipes and
handed one to each boy. "There y'are.
Good 'unting, old boys." The overwhelming
sweetness of the discharged gases made old
Dad sniff scornfully, but the boys lapped it
luxuriously. They lay on the floor, their
coats serving as pillows, and followed the
amiable meditations upon the flesh which the
hop invoked.

As they lay there, the younger of the two,
called Perce, his face already assuming a
parchment surface after three years of the
pipe, watched Twinkletoes as she fluttered
about the workshop. His eyelids drooped.
His eyes became as the bright blue beads of
the lamps: pin-points of phosphorescence.
His fingers curled at the bamboo stem of his

41

pipe. He absorbed the lyrical flow of her upright figure, and the chiming colors of her dress, and the swift play of her apple-blossom arms. The meaning behind his gaze could no more be interpreted than the thought behind a cat's eyes.

Just then the latch lifted. Dad darted round with a movement of apprehension that would have puzzled Twinkletoes had she seen it. Chuck Lightfoot walked in. As he entered he caught the smoker's fixed stare. He said nothing, but his nose twitched.

"Got the boodle?" Dad asked.

Chuck grunted. "A few. I planted a lot more up West. Met Wallopy and Pimlico Pete. Pete took some, and Wallopy wangled the big 'uns. They got away with it all right."

"Good biz. That'll be greens for dinner. 'Ave a cup of you-and-me? I'm hashing some up here."

"Righto."

"This new lot's the goods, ain't it?" Dad

42

went on, as he fussed round a kettle on a gas-ring. "Got 'em where we want 'em."

"Yerss. I don't think they'll ramp us on this lot."

Twinkletoes paid no attention to the technical conversation, but when it was ended she swung round.

" 'Ullo, Chuck. Where you going to sit?"

"Oh, I don't care. On the bench, if you like." He sprang up to the bench, and Twinkletoes clambered up beside him, where they faced the pipe men, who now lay with closed eyes breathing like a farmyard. Twinks lit a cigarette and puffed it ecstatically. Chuck's face was downcast; the presence of Twinkletoes, and her kindly comradeship, flicked him on the raw. He was suffering his daily hell.

Innocent of his agony, Twinkletoes chipped him. The genius of mischief bubbled in her blood and boiled over in glances and movements. "Brace up, old son! Why the glumness? Why the bad looks? Why

43

the hell the sad step? Cough up to your
Twinks the whenceness of it all? Lost your
money and found a last year's sweep-ticket—
what?"

Chuck grunted.

"Never mind, old son. Life's a game. It's
an adventure, and it's worth having whether
it's gay or sad. Ain't it, now? You look
as cheerful as a wet funeral on early closing
day. I ain't feeling too good to-night, but
I ain't sucking lemons about it. I was coming along Mandarin, and that blasted old
Adnitt woman was torturing that kiddie
again. I wish I was strong. I'd put her
through it. What'd you do, Chuck, if you
see anyone beating a kid?"

"Eh?" Chuck looked up sharply. His
glance swerved to the slumbering Perce.
"Why, I reckon I'd—I'd break their blasted
face in."

Twinkletoes looked raptly at him. Her
fury against the suffering of the helpless,
with admiration for this champion of the

44

helpless, blazed in her eyes, "Yes, and you could do it, too, couldn't you, Chuck? I see you fight once—round at Battling's ring."

"If I see anyone 'urting a child," said Chuck slowly, "no one wouldn't need to show me what to do." He looked at Twinkletoes. "If there's one thing that gets my goat it's——"

The latch clicked. Hank Hogan walked in, his slippery air and slippery clothes giving him the manner of a disgraced eel. Dad, who was noisily swigging tea in the corner, looked up.

"Like to see you for a minute—private-like," said Hank.

"All right, old son. Down yeh go."

They descended to the basement. This was a small cellar, lit by three green-shaded lamps. Wisps of crinkled paper lay about the floor and on the bench. There were test-tubes and a retort and many small bottles.

45

Hank chewed a piece of plug reflectively.

"Just seen the Pearly Prince," he remarked.

"So?"

"Um." He continued chewing for a minute. "Got something big on just now. On'y he ain't got the right things."

"So?"

"Um. There's a good thing for the chap who can get 'em for 'im."

"There ought to be."

"Oh, Pearly alwis does things proper. He's got the specifications and all that; but he can't put 'is 'and on the right chap. Chap who's got the plant and who can keep quiet."

"Yerss," said Dad slowly. "It ain't so easy."

"Well," snapped Hank decisively. "Got me?"

Dad looked squarely at him with a blank expression. "Nothing doing."

"What! Mean t' say you ain't on?"

"Just that."

46

"Well, of all the blasted—— D'you re'lize what's in it? Pearly'll go two 'underd for the right things. And you can do 'em as *easy*——" He swept a tired, ragged arm round the cellar. "Why, it's like falling orf a log. With this lay-out you could—— 'Ere, you gorn barmy?"

"Nit."

"Well, ain't a couple of 'underd enough for yeh? There ain't no risk. You know Pearly. Pearly's straight."

"That's so. Pearly's all right. I ain't saying nothing 'bout Pearly. But this ain't my lay."

"Oh? What's got yeh? Got bugs—or what?"

"No. Only——" He looked round, bent towards Hank, and lowered his voice. "I ain't saying two 'underd won't be useful. But I can't make it in that way."

"Oh. Blasted partic'ler, ain't yeh?"

"'Ank, y'know my Twinkletoes?"

"Um. What about 'er?"

47

"Well . . . you know . . . if you 'ad a kid like that, would you like to run risks to do anything—know what I mean, anything dirty-like.

"Teeth and testimonials! What you bin doing these last four years?"

" 'At's different. I 'ad to. To give 'er 'er chance. Don't think I've enjoyed it, 'Ank. Don't think I ain't gone through a good bit of 'ell over it. Wondering if she'd ever find out. You know what she is— straight as they make 'em. Clean as if she'd come from 'eaven. An' it's alwis bin my line to live up to 'er. But I 'ad to give 'er 'er chance. And this was the only way. Well, she's 'ad 'er chance, and she's made good; and I'm pretty near ready to quit. I 'ad to make just that bit o' money some'ow, and I made it. She's earning three quid a week now with the Quayside Kids, and I ain't got no need to make no more money this way. We're comfortable and 'appy, and what'd 'appen if she knew, Christ only

48

knows. It don't bear thinking about. You'd understand that, 'Ank, if she was your kid. If you lived with 'er you'd *'ave* to live straight and clean. You couldn't do no other way. She's like that. I can't explain. It's just there; she has that effeck on yeh. Now I've started 'er, I'm going to quit. The die-stamping business is moseying along all right, and wiv what she earns we're quite comfy.

"So that's that. I'm going to quit. Tell Pearly. 'E's a good chap, but I can't touch it. Straight, I can't. If I make money now I'm going to make it clean. See?"

"Ar. I dessay you're right. She's a great kid, your Twinks. But a couple of 'underd's a couple of 'underd—alwis will be. There ain't no risk. It could be just a last flutter, and it'd be nice to 'ave a little egg to put in the straight business, eh?"

"Nothing doing, Hank."

"Oh, awright. Don't let me shove it

49

dahn yer throat. I only put it your way, friendly-like, 'cos I thought you might be glad of a bit and 'cos I knew that the Prince'd trust you where he wouldn't no one else. But there y'are. That's alwis the way. Do a pal a turn——"

"That's all right, 'Ank. I know. I ain't sniffing at you. You're all right. But I just can't touch it, 'Ank. I've made the bit I 'ad to make, and there we are. Understand, don't yeh? There ain't no ill feeling about it. I 'preciate your bringing it to me —reely, I do."

"Awright. I s'pose you know yer own mind. I'll be shoving along. The Prince won't 'alf be sick, though."

"Oh, you can fix it somewhere else. Some of the Stepney boys'll take it on. Well, so long, 'Ank."

"So long."

They climbed the ladder to the main workshop.

As Dad's head appeared on the floor level,

there came a sharp scream in Twinkletoes' voice.

Pushing open the door, he saw her on the steps leading to the street. Reaching from his pillow on the floor, Perce the smoker had grabbed her ankle. She tumbled from the top step and fell upon him in a storm of skirts and curls. Dad saw two bright brown boots flash across the shop. One of these was lifted and came full on Perce's face. He howled and slackened his grip. Chuck, the owner of the brown boots, lifted Twinkletoes with reverent hands, and drew her aside.

"I'm all right," she gasped. "Don't bother, Chuck. He's a bit dopey, I reckon. I ain't funked of 'im any end up. Got bugs. He didn't mean it."

Dad leapt up the ladder, and Hank followed him. He glared upon the dithering, whining Perce. The tenderness and the jollity were gone from him. Something had happened to his Twinkletoes. But his mien was mild against that of Chuck, who stood over the culprit. A terrible white fire burned in his face, as austerely passionate as that which might have transformed the Man who drove sacrilegious intruders from the Temple.

He turned to Twinkletoes, who stood airily aloof. "Better run along, else yeh'll be late."

"Righto. Don't bother about it. It wasn't anything. I'm just off, Dad. See you after the show."

She ran to Dad and kissed him, and flitted through the door.

The men remained in awkward silence for a few moments.

"Well, I'll be off," said Hank. The atmosphere seemed constrained. He hated scenes, and he was afraid a scene was coming. "I'll be in the Lantern 'fyou want me—if you change yer mind, old cock."

"Righto."

When he had gone, Dad walked over to the sprawling Perce, and kicked him.

52

"Ought to be blasted well ashamed of yesself, you ought," he said. "You—putting yer nasty dirty mawlers on my kiddie. If you want to play games like that, find another shop. See?" His anger was inflamed by his own words. "You touch a—a youngster like that—you, yeh dirty little hop-toad. Bung off. See? Bung off. Quick, too, else me and you'll 'ave a row. Won't we, Chuck?"

But Chuck said nothing. He stared cataleptically.

The other smoker, who had been an indolent witness of the affair, rose, put on his coat, and searched for his hat.

"Nothing more, guv'nor?"

"No, nothing more. D'you see what young Perce was up to?"

"Sure. But then, he never could take his hop without going buggy. If a chap can't take his dose prop'ly he ought to drop it. Night."

Perce, too, found his feet and fumbled

53

with his coat, while Dad glowered upon him. He slithered up the steps, and out, as one conscious of wrong-doing, unwilling to admit it, too afraid to utter defiance.

Chuck watched him go. He stretched his arms widely, in apparent weariness.

"Well, I'll be toddling. See you in the Lantern, guv'nor."

"Toodle-oo, lad."

In the street, Chuck looked swiftly to right and left. Then he ran towards Mandarin Court. Perce was slinking round the corner. Chuck's hand fell like a bar of finely tempered steel on his shoulder.

He jumped idiotically; wriggled; then wailed.

"Leggo! Leggo!"

"I want you." He dragged him into the court. "Put 'em up."

"Eh?"

"Put 'em up."

"Whaffor?"

"You know what for."

54

"Grr yeh! Lemme go!"

"Going to put 'em up?"

"Grr! Bloody plucky, ain't yeh? I know your sort. Alwis wanter fight wiv fellers who don't train, just 'cos you're a pro. Wanter fight me 'cos yeh know I can't fight, and it's a sorf thing for yeh. Why don't yer fight the pros., eh?"

"Shut up. I'll fight *you* any way yeh like —feet, if yeh like. But I'm going to learn yeh. See? I'll learn yeh to put yer hands on—on 'er. I'll learn yeh. Going to put 'em up?"

Perce writhed, hesitated. Then shot a swift boot at Chuck's shins. With the sickness of the blow Chuck went down. For a moment only, though; then the face of Twinkletoes came before him, and he saw again the soiling hand of Perce about her holy person. In one movement he came from the ground and carried his left to Perce's nose. He did not hit hard, or Perce would have been out; indeed, he had to

55

maneuver to avoid landing on the point. He had no wish to use his skill or extend himself. He wanted to learn him.

"'Ave that to go on with, Perce," he snapped. "That'll learn yeh t'interfere with kids. Ain't yeh sorry yeh touched 'er—eh?"

Perce answered nothing. He ducked his head and made a dive to butt Chuck amidships. Chuck side-stepped and rattled his head with half-arm jabs, one-two, one-two. Perce went down, and lay kicking.

"Get up!"

"Sha'n't!"

Chuck grabbed his collar, pulled him to his feet, and beetled upon him. Then he worked the ding-dong on him with open palms, until the houses swam and the stars curveted in the sky. Perce staggered to the wall, and stood hunched up, mouthing fearful oaths about Chuck and Twinkletoes. Chuck listened attentively, then sent three smart ones to the dirty mouth.

"Say that again. Mention 'er name again,

56

and you won't 'ave a mouth to speak with. Understand?"

He bent over the crouching figure, prodding him in the ribs, sending half-arm jabs to the hidden face, and kneeing him about the body. Perce was gasping. He was bleeding from nose and mouth. His face was discolored to the tinge of raw beetroot.

By this time a bunch of loungers had gathered. Perce had no fight in him, and, to the delight of the company, Chuck, with very serious manner, tucked him under his arm and chastised him well and truly. They formed a circle and chanted a music-hall chorus of the day:

> "Dear old pals,
> Jolly old pals,
> You find where'er you roam!"

"That's that," he said, when it was ended. " 'F you want any more, y'know 'ow to get it. 'Tain't 'ealthy for you t'interfere with kids. See?"

Cissie Lightfoot, seated at her window

with a copy of *The Bouquet Novelettes* in her hand, witnessed the fight and, later, when Chuck and the crowd had departed, she called to the damaged Perce to step up.

He stepped up.

"What's my old pot-and-pan bin doing to yer?" she asked.

"Damn silly thing t'ask. Cancher see?"

"Yes, but what's it all for?"

"Oh, I d'know. They've all gorn barmy at the Works, I think. Anybody'd think that old Minasi's kid was Gawd's own angel."

Cissie became keen. She asked no questions for fear of getting evasive or inadequate answers.

"I know. Chuck's gorn batty over 'er. I've 'eard a lot in different ways. If she is a blasted angel—and it ain't so sure—kid's like her gen'ly know a bit—what the 'ell do they want to keep 'er 'ere for? In Poplar? We ain't got no room for angels 'ere. 'Eaven's their place. Why can't they keep in it? They on'y make trouble in a place like this." She looked through the grimy window, with its rag of curtain. "So Chuck put it acrors you? Tried to start on me t'other night, but it didn't come orf."

"Whaffor?"

"Oh, I chipped 'im about the nipper."

"Huh!" Perce gave a superior but rueful laugh. "I did a bit more than that. I'd bin 'aving a pipe, and I went bald-'eaded at 'er. Bald-'eaded. 'Strewth, y'ought t'ave seen the rumpus old Minasi and Chuck made. If I'd a-sold the business to the narks they couldn't 'a' bin madder. Well, I got one in fer Chuck, now, and I don't mind tellin' yeh even if 'e is yer 'usband."

"Oh, that don't worry me. Wish to Gawd 'e wasn't. I don't blame yeh. You got reason to."

"Yerss, and I'll work it orf 'fore long."

Cissie looked at him, and he at Cissie. "I s'pose, now . . ." she began.

"Yerss?"

"Oh—nothing."

59

"But you was saying . . ."

"Oh, I was on'y thinking. 'Ow easy it'd be. They're a rotten lot round there. All of 'em. Playing up to the angel-face like they was a blasted lot of parsons, and all the time doing—well, you know what. I ain't never been connected with games o' that sort. My people was respectable, and I've kept meself respectable."

She inspected her broken shoes.

"'At's so." Perce assumed boredom.

After a minute she looked up. "Plenty of people'd like to jump the game. Know old Territon?"

"What—th' Inspector?"

She nodded.

"'Ere—go easy," he snapped, and moved suddenly and sat down again, touching sore places with solicitous hands. "That'd be 'ealthy fer me, wouldn't it?"

"You could make a get-away 'forehand. You could lie under easy. I could fix it for yeh. I know a man."

Twinkletoes

"Grr!"

"Straight. Listen." She closed the window delicately. "Listen. You got one on Chuck. Well, I got a 'underd on 'im. Ain't I 'ad enough from 'im for the last six months? You don't know what I've 'ad. I've 'ad enough to—to—— And it's all through that lousy Minasi kid." Her face lost its slackness and became hard. Her hands closed. "I'd like to break 'em up. The whole lot. Break 'em. Smash 'em to bits. But I can't break 'em on me own. There's on'y one way I know, and if I used that . . . Y'see, people'd talk if I jumped me own man's game. Somebody else could, though, and me not know nothing about it, like. See what I mean? But there—I s'pose you're too funky to risk it. Besides . . ."

" 'Ere, come," said Perce airily. He preened himself. "I dunno so much about that. I ain't a fighter, I know. I ain't 'ad no training. But there ain't many things I'm afraid of. If I like to go for a thing, I

go—all out. Nobody who knows me'd say
that I funked. Not when I'm really keen.
Ask anybody. Ask old——"

"Well, then. You got yer chance. I'm
giving it yeh. You won't wipe Chuck out
by fighting. But . . ."

"Yerss."

"Well, then . . ."

They sat on rickety chairs in some minutes'
silence. Then: " 'Ave a drop o' beer," said
Cissie. "You look as though you could do
with it."

"I don' mind. And yeh needn't rub it in.
I feel like a plurry clothes-'orse."

"I know. 'Ere's luck! And now listen
to me."

And she kept him in cold, busy talk for the
space of an hour.

IV

ONCE out of Mandarin Court, Twinkletoes ran fawn-like towards the Quayside at Shadwell. She was late. The Quayside was a small affair that choked a byway of Commercial Road East —a dusty survival of the old-style hall, with a public-house adjoining. It had few turns on its books, and these came round in rotation every five or six weeks. But the Quayside public was pathetically faithful to its second-rate entertainers. One of the favorite turns was that of "The Quayside Kids," a troupe of juveniles led by Twinkletoes, who sang and danced; and a brave picture they made, those groups of glorious girls, touched with all the charms of their little years, with Twinkletoes in the centre, her young throat quivering like a singing bird's. Merely to gaze upon them was at once refreshment of body and spirit.

She was never quite placed by her audience. She drew them while some of them

—the bar crowd—resented being drawn.
They would leave their drinks to watch her
dances, fairy or goblin; and when she had
finished they would wonder why on earth
they'd left the bar. Yet, whatever she was—
angel or goblin or just a child—none could
be in her presence without gaining from her
something of that tranquillity of soul which
makes life not bearable but 'a magnificent
enterprise. At fifteen she knew all those
terrible things that philosophers achieve when
they come home by Weeping Cross. The
wisdom and the heart-ache, the tears and the
laughter, and the grief and beauty of all
transient things she carried in that pert head
set so aptly upon her, and her impetuous legs
translated to her people the glory of their
grey lives. The hearts of men and women
were entangled in her hair, and their desires
jangled with the anklets about her lily feet.

She taught them, without teaching, to
look tenderly upon everything. She taught
them that nothing was common or unclean

save cruelty and meanness. She taught them to be afraid of nothing but themselves. She made sweet and desirable all things that finer people called Vulgar. She ridiculed everything, and her laughter never hurt; it was like sun and rain falling from the sky to cleanse and clothe. She taught them to live boldly and gladly, making beauty where no beauty was, and her shining creed of "Ain't people and things lovely?" lit the monotonous hours wherever she carried it.

Sometimes she danced like the happy little girl that she was, and sometimes in a simulated frenzy of adult passion and despair.

She would dance on for her solo with an air of tragic portent, which she shattered with the first flash of her smile. Folks felt at times that she was a poem; and then, by her flagrant gaiety, that she was a crackling epigram. Certainly she was a problem; not a problem to ponder, but a problem, like life, to accept and enjoy.

Her stage manner embraced all; yet re-

mained curiously private and personal. She
would turn suddenly and deliver to the stalls
a glance at once wide and intimate. All
were in the joke, yet each felt that he alone
understood it. She was in raptures about
some marvellous secret, apart from the business of the stage, and she possessed that
intangible something that wafted this rapture across the band to each individual in the
steaming house. So unerring was her
judgment in regard to her own .capacities
that, when she wished to feature a particular
dance, the controller of the troupe usually
allowed it, and a small and dusty hall in the
Shadwell district once presented Twinkletoes
and companions in the sombre *Valse Triste*
of Sibelius. Draped in a black veil, she
sleep-walked through its long surging
strokes. They evoked in her a certain mys-
tery into which the real child dissolved and
through which one glimpsed a new, remote
Twinkletoes; and a breath of foreign North-
ern seas was carried to East End working

men and women. Again, she might choose
stately pavanes and minuets, joyous gavottes
and mazurkas, frantic sarabands. But
most she loved and danced those crystalline
bits of Mediterranean melody from Mas-
senet, Delibes, Giordano, Wolf-Ferrari,
Ponchielli, and Scarlatti: music which ran
into her pulses and made her body a very
tune.

To the gallery boys, who had constituted
themselves a guard of honor to the Quayside
Kids, she was a pet. There existed between
them and her a subtle *rapprochement,* and
the symphony for the Kids' number was
greeted with yells and local war-cries. At the
rise of the curtain she would acknowledge
this greeting, sometimes with a delicious
grimace, sometimes, when she felt devilish,
with a raspberry. They liked her, not so
much for her turn (they would have told you
that dancing bored them stiff), as because
she was so lovely to look at, her joy so con-
tagious. They had loved her since the night

of the alarm of fire, when she had averted a panic by dancing on before a front cloth and distributing her garters and ribbons to the stalls, while chi-iking the gallery with ribald comment and richly improper gesture.

If, in her dance, she showed signs of flagging, they would encourage her: "Go it, young 'un. Faster! Put yer back in it! Put rings round 'em, kid!" When the Kids' turn was over, and Twinkletoes took her curtain call, there would come from the boys a harmonized chorus:

Are we to part like this, Bill?
Are we to part this way?

For any turn that failed to reach their standard—red-nose comedian, piano entertainer, or girl vocalist—they had a set formula. Taking the signal from their leader, they would chant, to the four notes of Big Ben:

Git orf! Git orf!
Git orf! Git orf!

Then, in staccato shouts:

We—— Want——

and explosively:

TWINKLETOES!
We—— Want——
TWINKLETOES!

and this they would maintain until the disconcerted artist had disappeared.

As she pelted towards the stage-door she was greeted and chi-iked from all sides. A group of little girls hung round the door, enviously worshipping all members of the Quayside Kids, and particularly Twinkletoes, while they dreamed of the day when they, too, might get "on the stage" and possess that glory and power that enabled them to pass casually through that narrow, frowsty gateway into the delectable land of lights and colors and popular acclaim. People stopped what they were doing to give a nod, and did nothing for some moments after, following her with glances as she went. The landlady of the Quayside bar beamed upon her. The pot-man chirruped a "Watcherkid!" The stage-door keeper turned laborious wit upon her, and in the dressing-room the Quaysides received her with shrill whistles, while the Matron in charge of them, a stout old dame in black dress and white apron, met her with placid reproof:

"You're late, Minasi!"

"Can't 'elp it, Ma. Just in time. Be just in time and fear not." And then her little body was a whirl of frock and petticoat and descending stockings. "Who's got me powder? Where's me powder? Suffering Jesus! Someone's pinched me——"

"Minasi!" cried Ma.

"No, but, Ma—someone's bin and 'alf-inched me powder. Someone's done the dirty on me. Never mind. I'd sooner have a red nose than a spot on——"

A call-boy appeared.

70

"Quaysides! Willie Wangler's on."

Meanwhile, at hundreds of late tea-tables in Limehouse and Poplar, people were anticipating a visit to the Quayside. Husbands were putting on clean shirts and otherwise preparing to take their wives. Bright boys were cleaning their boots and arranging to meet their girls at given corners in order to have sixpenn'orth of "lean-over." Women with the evening free were planning entertainment with other women. They talked of it; they thought about it; they washed and arranged for it. Many of them had saved money for it, or denied themselves a relish for tea in order to obtain one of the more expensive seats. They disinterred Sunday bonnets and speculated as to whether they might wear the everyday one or whether that Mrs. So-and-so might be there, quizzing; and they were robed and ready half-an-hour before they should start.

Why? Because Twinkletoes and the children were dancing; and, because it was

71

the spirit of youth that they danced, all the old ladies of Poplar crowded to see it.

At the theatre they inspected the faded photographs, hung at the main entrance, of the massed troupe of joyous children posed in a finale, and the separate photographs of Twinkletoes, and then joined the queues, at pit and gallery doors.

Willie Wangler, the famous washer-woman comedian, was the star, but the Quay-side Kids were the bottom-liners, and of the eager multitude only the young people were attracted by Willie Wangler.

The evening's bill was discussed in detail, arbitrary criticism being offered on each turn, with occasional exclusive information as to the personal habits of any given turn.

"Well, I 'ope they open the door soon. My feet's that cold. I alwis love to see the kids dancing, don't you? Ain't they little darlings? And they do seem to enjoy it so."

"Ah, that's a fact they do—especially

that golden-'eaded one—Twinkletoes, I believe they call 'er. I know somebody who
knows 'er."

"No. Reely?"

"Ah. And they do say she's just the same
in private life as she is on the stage."

"There, now. You don't say so. Y'know
I've alwis 'eard that they're very cruel to
children on the stage when they're training
'em. But cert'ny this lot don't look it."

"No fear. It don't do to believe all you
read in the papers, my dear."

Directly the call-boy gave the warning
that Willie Wangler was on, Ma made a
determined assault on Twinkletoes. In her
arms she carried a cloud of filmy, colored
stuffs. She grabbed the child and, with
deft fingers, pulled at laces and buttons, until
the growing pile of clothes blossomed about
her ankles like a rose. Through the single
garment she now wore, her limbs rippled and
shone like flames. She stood upright before
Ma, her movements and glances swift as a

startled bird's, her arms stretched to slip into the robe for which the old woman fumbled, her body eager and clean and poised like a deer for the leap. The several curls hung like crops of golden wine, and every fibre of her seemed to tingle with delight. She was an ecstasy of youth.

Face, bosom, neck, arms and shoulders were quickly powdered or rouged; then Ma took up a mass of orange-tinted silk. One end she gave to Twinkletoes, and herself walked away unwinding as she went.

"Ready?" asked Twinkletoes. She put one end under her arms, then, turning and turning her gleaming body, she moved towards Ma, entwining her person in silk, unwinding herself here and there and winding anew to avoid creases. This ceremony ended, strips of blue silk were wound about her bare arms and lily legs, and over all she put a green frock edged with fur at neck, wrists and hem.

When she was fully encased, Ma shoved

74

her into a chair, and tended her curls, though she had already dressed them at home, and drenched them with a fluid that left a peaceful perfume of violets. Then she turned her about, took her bare legs upon her lap and slipped morsels of cotton wool under the soles, and wound strips of tape about them and the ankles before fitting scarlet stockings and ballet shoes.

In five minutes Twinkletoes was ready for the first number, the bright green frock and scarlet stockings covering the gauze necessary for a Puck dance, so that she could peel the top frock and stockings in the wings while Ma powdered her legs, and be ready for the next number in a few seconds. The girls waited in alert idleness. Some of them were older than Twinkletoes and a little too hardened in the coarser usages of life. Twinkletoes did not dislike them for their ways; they hurt nobody but themselves, and they were otherwise such darlings; but their frolics made no great appeal to her.

A mature girl of seventeen came across to her.

"Say—Twinks—Roseleaf's going to give a jag after the show. Come along? Why not? You never have."

"Not for me, thanks."

"Why not? 'Squite all right. Old Roseleaf's nothing to be afraid of. He gets a bit fresh at times, but you can always barge him off. We're going to the Lantern—downstairs—and then move on to the other place. Go on. Spread yourself a bit and come. It's awful fun."

"No, thanks, Lilac. 'Tain't my game."

"Oh, you *are* a snuffer. Why ever not? I know you'd enjoy it. We only have wine, and I've seen you put down plenty of that."

"No, I'm not coming. I'd like to, but—it don't seem—oh, I dunno. I can't come. Thanks, Lilac."

Lilac inspected her. Then continued in her clipped accent which marked her from the

76

others as a girl of some education: "What d'you mean?"

"Oh, well," in a burst of confidence, "it's my dad, y'know. 'E wouldn't like it."

"What's that matter? My dad wouldn't neither, if he knew. Only I don't let him know. I tell him we've had a rush rehearsal after the show. He doesn't know any better."

"Ah, yes, but my dad ain't like that. I couldn't never tell 'im a lie."

"Oh, what's a lie—once in a way?"

"Ah, you don't understand. My dad's different. 'E ain't ordinary. I'd feel a dirty beast if ever I told 'im a lie."

"Ghu! All dads are like. What's yours? He's only——"

"My dad's the finest, straightest man in the world," shrilled Twinkletoes, jumping up from her chair. " 'E's one o' the best men that ever lived, and anyone who says 'e ain't is asking for a mouthful o' blood. Suffering Je——"

77

"Minasi!" cried Ma. "You know the rules about swearing."

" 'E's the cleanest thing that ever was," she continued, with dislocating fervor, "and I'm not coming on your old jags. 'E wouldn't think it decent. I dunno what 'e'd think o' me if 'e 'eard. 'E ain't never done anything dirty 'imself, and 'e'd think this dirty. I know 'e would. And that's all about it. It's good enough for me. I know what goes on there. I ain't a fool, Lilac. I know the rules of the game from soup to nuts. If you 'ad a dad like mine you'd understand. I don't say I wouldn't like to come. I would. I've often got all feathered up, like I'd give anything to go on the bat for a bit with your lot, but some'ow when I think of my dad I just can't. Y'see, 'e's clean all through. 'E don't understand these jag games, and if I batted I'd feel like I couldn't never go near 'im again."

"Oh, all right. You needn't get your wool out over it."

"I wasn't. On'y—you see why I can't come in, and——"

"Quaysides, please!"

"Come on in, girls!" she cried. "The water's fine!"

The group of green children flittered down the stairs to the wings. Fat Markie Roseleaf, the manager, stood in a corner. He had a tawny skin that suggested negroid blood. Crude, indefinable emotions sped across his face, expressed in changing lines about the mouth, as he looked long and heavily at this cluster of youth.

V

"YOICKS! Yoicks! Yoicks!"

It was the voice of the nimble old Dad outside Twinkletoes' bedroom. In his hand he carried a cup of tea and a packet of Woodbines.

" 'Ark, 'olloa!" cried the sleepy dancer.

Dad walked in, placed the tea and cigarettes on a chair, with a box of matches, and stood looking with effervescent amusement at the tumbled bed and its sleep-flushed owner. Her eyes were bright and clear; her yellow curls running with a wayward fire. She grimaced at him.

"Marv'llous bloody kid, ain't you?" he chortled affectionately.

"Don't care if I am. I ain't kicking. What's the time?"

"Ar pars nine."

"Um." She sipped the tea, took a Woodbine, and lit it, and lay back on the pillow. Her little nightdress, disordered, showed a soft white shoulder on which still rested a

80

little of last evening's powder. She stretched her arms above her, and her sweet, straight body, perfect in its immaturity, like that of a white rosebud which suggests happier things than the full flower achieves, was vibrant. "Oh, Dad—ain't people and things lovely? I'm so 'appy."

"That's the style. Watcher doing to-day? I'm just orf to th' Works."

"Oh, I d'know. Mooning around, I s'pose. I'll pop round and see old Mrs. Toplady, I think. She's rather peeved just now. Take 'er some flowers and a drop of that old brandy; we got some left, I think. That ought to let the dog loose. She's been a dear old duck in 'er time, but no one goes near 'er now she's up against it."

"Righto."

"Seen my new silk stockings, old man? In that brown paper over there. Cast yer eye over 'em. Ain't they glad?"

Dad unfastened the parcel and inspected the flimsy arrangements.

81

"Huh! Looks as though only the best is good enough for you."

"Oh, I can rub along with the best if there ain't nothing better. Won't I have the cheery leg with them on? On'y bought 'em last night. You needn't look like that. They didn't cost what you think they did. I got 'em through Jessie. She's got an aunt at one of the big Stores, and gets everything cost price. Oh, look! Sun's coming out. Ain't everything good? Bung off, Dad. I'm going to get up. See you at th' Works 's evening. Don't go down the mine, Daddy; there's plenty of coal in the yard!"

She had an idle day before her: there was no rehearsal. She hated rehearsals as she hated everything of routine and order. She knew far better than the conductor how to interpret a given passage, and she had no use for his conventional theories. Too, rehearsal always started with blasphemy and ended with irritation and incipient neurosis.

While the conductor seldom got his own

way in the matter of Twinkletoes' solos, he would put the troupe through an ensemble forty or fifty times to get the effect he wanted. The work would end always with the same ceremony.

"Now, then, you perishers," he would snap, when at last some intricate movement was satisfactorily accomplished; "down on yer knees, the lot of yer."

Down they would go on the cold stage.

"Put yer 'ands together."

Twenty pairs of little hands would be folded as for prayer.

"Now, then: repeat after me: Oh, Gawd——"

"Oh, God——" they would pipe in solemn ritual.

"We thank Thee——"

"We thank Thee——"

"That Thou has sent——"

"That Thou has sent——"

"Dear Ernie Pugnutt——"

"Dear Ernie Pugnutt——"

83

"To drill us blasted lot of twicers into shape."

"To drill us blasted lot of twicers into shape."

"That's it. And now go and lose yourselves—quick. I 'ate the sight of yeh."

When Dad had gone, Twinkletoes played at getting up. In Shantung Place there were no baths, so she paddled and splashed in a washing basin and flung her delighted limbs; and her elfin face, her arms, like boughs of May, urgent and bright, and the most piquant legs in Poplar, all gave assurance, if any doubted, that everything was indeed lovely.

Always in her room was a bunch of violets, bought every day from the old woman at the corner of East India Dock Road, near the Star of the East. These were placed in a bottle on the washing-stand where she could see them from the bed when she woke.

"Silly of me," she once explained to Dad, "but I must pray to something, and I can't

84

pray to God. He seems such a long way off.
So I kneel down every night, and pray to
these. You can't pray properly to anything you can't catch hold of, like."

She dressed slowly, and with some care,
hesitating for a moment between brown
socks and the new silk stockings, finally
choosing the stockings and drawing them on
with a loud sigh of delight. The short frock
which finished aptly at the knee gave her
legs a brave show, and in their transparent
coverings they appeared positively insolent,
challenging. She quickly made the beds and
"tidied the place" up, leaving the heavier
cleaning for Mrs. Next-door, who came in
three times a week and turned the cottage
on its head. Dad took all his meals outside,
bringing in cooked meat for Twinkletoes'
supper, so that only on Sundays did she
have to do what she called the Domestic Act.

These jobs done, she found a brown sports
coat and a lacy hat, and was ready to astonish
the natives—as she always did. In the

kitchen she filled a small bottle with a measure of the old brandy for Mrs. Toplady, and poured herself out a small Bass— her customary breakfast.

She paused for a moment at the door to finish her third cigarette, tossing back the crowding curls, a petulant leg kicking idly at nothing. Then with a thrill of dainty frock she skipped into Shantung Place, whose ladies were "sloshing down their fronts," as they said, and gave the merry word to all she passed.

She loved the comradeship of streets and shops, and hated the silly old country. The lights and the noise and the pungent odors held her happily captive. A farm was to her an abode of blood and filth. The damnable solitudes, the enervating skies, the stupid seas and woods and fields, she loathed. She was a town girl, and sweeping moorlands and flower-spangled hills lit in her, as in all town people, pernicious flames, while the considered allurements of town life, which

86

abounded for the having in Limehouse, had left her unmarked. The life she led might be labelled by some as artificial. But among theaters and halls, sensuous music, swirling limbs, provocative song, glitter, drinking-bars, smoking-rooms, and the appurtenances, in the popular conception, of moral dirt and the soul's decay, she developed towards joy. Being very wise, she knew that the only natural life for humans is town life; that spaces and silences are unnatural, and therefore encourage the development of the unnatural. She knew that country life is fundamentally obnoxious to man, and only serves to drive him stupid or into himself, and sets him seeking in strange corners that distraction that is ever at hand in comfortable streets. God created man in a fair and lonely garden, she maintained; but He never meant him to stay there, or that jolly old parable about Ten Talents wouldn't have been told.

Her first move was towards a low lane

of crumbling cottages behind Poplar High Street. Its aroma was offensive. Betel nut and decaying refuse battled with each other. One looked from the windows of these cottages into the bleary face of Poplar, and the vociferant life of the main road came clearly, in tabloid form. The walls of the houses were peeling in dank strips. Slatternly women of indeterminate ages lounged in doorways, gossiping with Next-door, or thrusting heads from frowsy windows to cry philosophies to Over-the-road. A cat's-meat cart stood at the corner, and Twinkletoes stopped her progress to stroke the head of the dolorous horse.

" 'Ullo, 'ere's a norse. What a nice norse! Poor old norsey-porsey. 'Ave a banana? I ain't got one, but you could 'ave one if I 'ad."

A half-starved child, of nine lean winters, stood with nose pressed against the window of a cheap sweet and cake shop. Twinkletoes looked at her. Then she gave her a

88

violent shove in the back. The child's lunatic start showed that she had reason to fear such approaches.

Twinkletoes jerked a thumb at the window with one of her rich grimaces which asked a question or told a story without words. She opened the door and went in, and the child, understanding, followed her. Twinkletoes whistled on her teeth and jangled coppers before her guest.

"Cakes, dear," said Twinkletoes to the grey-haired dame of the shop. "And choco-late. And one o' those hot drinks. . . . There y'are kid. Bung off. Think kindly of me when I'm dead."

With stolid face the child took the gifts, looked up at Twinkletoes, then turned from the shop, and fled furiously down the street towards home.

As Twinkletoes proceeded to Mrs. Top-lady's, a neat, spry figure came smartly round a corner, conscious of the glories of bowler hat, cigarette, and wanghee cane.

His lively face conveyed the awful suggestion that he was about to be funny.

" 'Ullo, Face!" said Twinkletoes.

He stopped. The cigarette, riding so
jauntily on his lips, dropped. He fumbled
wildly for it, caught it, squashed it against
him, then left it to its fate. It went miser-
ably to the gutter in a shower of sparks, and
Twinkletoes wondered if glow-worms looked
like that when you trod on them.

"Oh—you—Swankpot. Bin to the second-
'and shop. I see." He pointed to the
stockings.

"Yes. Met your father there—pawning
some of the hats what 've got too small for
you."

"Huh! Fresh thing ain't you? . . .
'Aven't 'eard 'bout me, I s'pose?"

"That's all we do 'ear about when you
start talking."

"No—serious. Roseleaf's going to give
me a trial."

"Oh. 'Ope 'e finds you guilty."

90

"No, reely, though. No chipping, Twinks. 'E's going to give me a show. Extra turn. Sat'd'y night. Imitations, and song and dance."

" 'Onest? Well, 'ope you come through all right, Bert. I'll get in early, and see you. Don't get nervy. 'F you go as you did at that smoking concert, you're all right. Goo' luck, boy."

"Thanks, kid. S'long."

" 'Ow's yer father?"

"Oh, 'e's all right. On'y 'e don't like this strike o' mine. Silly of 'im, y'know. But I don' take no notice. I just go on, and let 'im growse. I got to get on, y'know, some'ow. There ain't nothing in that warehouse place for me. I got to move some'ow. . . . Y'see 'e thinks I shall get on top and —sort of look down on 'im, but that ain't me. 'Is little bats don't worry me. 'E's always the old dad. I ain't going to ask him to get on with me, if 'e don't want to. But I sha'n't ever get orf 'im. That ain't my style.

91

Stick to them what sticks to you is my motter. Well—wow-wow!"

Twinkletoes went on, and found Mrs.
Toplady in a chair in the kitchen of her cottage. Her eyes glistened at sight of her
visitor. They became twin stars when she
saw the visitor's gift, and she remarked that
God was good to His own, bless 'Is 'eart.
She found a glass at once, and proceeded to
do herself good.

"My! but that's a drop of rare stuff,
Twinks, my love."

"You bet. Brown brandy, my dear.
Guaranteed to stretch the dog out at fifty
yards."

"Don't it drink lovely and smooth?"

"Yes, you don't want no didn't-oughter
with that, eh? Just met young Bertie Trundett. 'E's going to get a show at our place,
'e tells me."

"There, now! Ain't it wonderful 'ow the
children get on now'days? Wonderful.
Them Trundetts, now. Brought up in the

gutter, as you might say, and now they got a piano."

"Got it on the 'ire system, though" said a ragged voice, through Mrs. Toplady's kitchen window. " 'Cos I know the shop they got it at, and I seen 'im paying the instal ——That's a nice drop o' stuff you got there, Mrs. Toplady." The intruder sniffed approvingly.

"Yes," said Mrs. Toplady, "and there s on'y enough for one."

"Oh, awright. Awright. I ain't one to shove meself. I can take a 'int, same as others. I know when I ain't wanted."

"Never mind, old dear," cried Twinkletoes, as the visitor disappeared into her own grounds, "I'll bring you some next time— a real nice drop."

"There, now!" said the visitor to the eternities. "Ain't she a bleeding little angel?"

Twinkletoes, brave little woman, was regarded as a court of appeal in this lost lane, and was received with that courtesy which in more polite parts is reserved for the vicar or the district visitor, though here the vicar and his ladies seldom dared to show themselves. Even the solitary constable found his casual gazes at loungers met with an easy brute calm which disturbed his self-assurance. Twinkletoes mothered the Lane's children, when she had time. She advised as to the expenditure of the few shillings that arrived on Saturday nights. She knew by instinct where the best value was to be obtained; the right stall in the right street when potatoes were in question, and how one should come at the highest value in the matter of fried fish. By graphic parables, she had induced Mrs. Trundett to abandon her ineffectual fumblings at spotting the winner; and for those to whom he was an urgent necessity, she had found the ideal Uncle.

She looked in at the Trundetts' to congratulate them on Bert's coming debut, and found herself involved in a domestic up-heaval.

"Say, Twinkletoes, wonder if you'd mind popping in next door and having a say at them. Way 'e knocks 'er about's something awful. Up against the wall. Fair shook my ornaments orf the mantelpiece t'other night. It did, straight. And they cost money. I bought 'em meself. At the six-penny-'apney shop. So you can tell."

Next door, Mr. Bill Garside hulked in a chair by the fire, his feet on the hob, his mouth at a brown stone jug.

"Hi—you!"

" 'Ullo, kid."

"Go easy on yer indoor sports, old cock."

"Talking to me?"

"Um. Hide-and-seek with Mrs. Garside's all right, but what about Mrs. Trundett's ornaments. Eh?"

"Well, what about 'em?"

"You smashed 'em. Bashing yer bother-and-strife's 'ead against the wall, you

95

knocked 'em off Mrs. T.'s mantelpiece."

"Oh. Sorry."

"I should think so. And why don't yeh wash yesself, yer twicer? You wouldn't 'alf cop it if I was yer wife."

"I bet I would. Gaw'd 'elp the bloke wot marries you. Like a mouthful of ginger and mustard, you are." He grinned as an amiable giant might grin at a furious elf.

"Now, look 'ere, me old brown son—do pull yesself together a bit. Go on. Just to please me." She put her arm round his chair, and did what she called her Soul's Awakening business.

"Oh, chuck it. Gwan away. Don' look at me like that, or, 'fore I know where I am, I shall be going to work." He shuddered.

"Well, why don't yeh? 'Tain't the game, y'know. Pretty to watch, sir, pretty to watch. But knocking the old thing about like that. . . . Apart from Next-door's ornaments. You are a slacking old perisher —reely you are."

"Gaw!" he chuckled, "don't the nippers talk to yeh, now? Wonder what I'd a-got if I'd talked to grown-ups like what you talk to me. You kids are getting too 'ot. You wanter bit o' strap. 'At's what you want."

"Wouldn't do me no good, old man. Might do you good, though. Go on—give us a kiss. And then give the ol' woman a kiss. And make it up with old Trundett. 'E ain't 'alf mad about 'is ornaments."

"What? That little bald-'eaded sardine? Why, I could eat 'im with 'alf me mouth. Well, nev' mind. 'Ere's yer kiss, little Pot-o'-mustard. And we'll see what happens o' Sat'd'y. If that thing I've backed comes 'ome, I'll give the ol' missis a fair treat. I will. I'll—I'll take 'er to the Quayside. And then we'll 'ave some fish-and-chips at Rosen's. There! That good 'nough for yer?"

"Old man Garside—you're a cracker. S'long."

She passed out and through the Lane.

97

"Bless 'er lovely 'eart," mumbled a toothless old dame, whose eyes carried a twinkle reflective of good days gone. There's a bleeding little saint for yeh, if ever Gawd made one."

From the cottages she went to Chinatown, where strolled or loitered the furtive Chinks. London's yellow streak—Limehouse Causeway and Pennyfields—is severed by the wide, flat West India Dock Road. Its quality is tasted before you reach it—the tang of spices, bilge-water, tarred ropes; the flavor of drugging flowers. It is just a quayside; a resting-place for sea-wanderers; and it holds that indefinable atmosphere of impending arrivals and departures.

Once a year the cold heart of the Orient makes merry, and it rings with the noise of revelry inflamed by Moi-kwee-lo, a gin distilled from rice and flavored with rose leaves and remote Asiatic buds. The Causeway is fully illuminated, throwing antic shadows from those who dance and frolic at the Feast of the Lanterns. Color and movement arrive; the adventurous uncertainty of shadow; mists; and unapproachable windows of many tones gleaming inscrutable messages. The sinister clashes with the silver-pensive. Always there are following feet: the firm feet of the constable; the bullying boots of the tough; the thick steps that trickle from the bars; and through all the whisper of slippers, and the rustling vocabularies of the Pacific.

Barbarous voices are raised, with appealing pipes of uncertain pitch, solemn gongs, and crackling fireworks. Musicians squat on tables, their proficient fingers fluttering over the strings of guitars like butterflies over honeyed flowers. They play apparently without a sense of time, but listening carefully one discovers that they take a few notes, juggle with them, and give them a certain twist and spin which creates form. *Yang-yow, yang-yow* go the instruments, and *Hao ye to!* go the nasal voices, and *Moh-li-Hwa!*

99

The shuttered aspect of the quarter never affrighted Twinkletoes. She held that she could put any old joker in his place; and she frequently did. Too, she knew the Chinese, and their kindly ways; she had nothing to fear from them. It was the scrofulous Malays of the quarter who menaced young children, and these she fixed with a careful eye when they passed her.

She walked boldly into the corner stores, chi-iked the boys who were hanging about the counter, and bought some suey-sen and lon-gans. While they were being packed she trotted round the shop, with its dried seaweed, dried strips of fish and duck, and bitter fruits, pulling down tins, examining everything that looked interesting, and climbing a ladder to the colored packets on the high shelves. The elegantly mustached proprietor looked fondly at her, and murmured: "Pao-pei!"

When the parcel was ready she departed with it to the little white café in the Causeway. "Must 'ave some grub," she assured herself. "Do you suffer from that sinking feeling? If so, send a postcard to Quong Sum." She mounted to the upper chamber, and seated herself unabashed among the oily seamen and the flusey white girls, who were teaching them the English language of physical love.

"Ao! Baitho!" the waiter sang to her, and she replied with:

"Wow-wow, old cock!"

With chop-sticks busily moving, she swallowed a couple of noodles and a chop-suey and a dish of chow-chow, and then lingered over her tea and dried chrysanthemum buds, luxuriously puffing a cigarette.

The sing-song girls looked at her uncomfortably. They knew her, and were a little afraid of her. She said and did such outrageous things for one so young; yet they felt that she was good, while wondering whether she were not secretly of the breed of themselves; and they could never be sure

101

of her; never, by any means, come at the truth for fear of being snubbed with horror of their questionings and behavior, of hearing their own minds and habits cut to pieces. They decided that she was best left alone. She was very sure of herself; lived only by her own laws—whatever they might be—and held and expressed independent opinions.

After her meal she went through the bead curtain to the kitchen, and sat among the cooking boys and talked to them in London-Chinese.

"'Ow goes ol fella-chap? All right?"

"Yeh. Ollight."

"You do heap plenty business to-day?"

"Yeh. Good. Heap tled. Plen binnizez."

"Make lot money?"

"Ho no. Not mek lot mully."

"Garn. You make heap more money'n Sing See in Pennyfields."

They shook their heads in slow deprecation.

"Sing See mek heap lot mully. We mek heap tled. No mek mully."

102

"Garn—chuck it. Say. Want tea-pot. Tea-pot. All same baby cradle. You know." She pointed to a tea-pot on a shelf, sunk in a wicker basket lined with soft cushions. " 'Ow much?"

"Twenny silling sispeh, my de-ah mess."

"No can."

"Fifteen silling."

"No can. Give five shilling."

"Ollight, my de-ah mess, I tek."

"Good. You come see me to-night Quay-side? See me dance?"

"No can. No mully."

"No want money. Me give ticket. See? Me give this. You come?"

"Ollight. I ken. You vay lice gel."

"Yes. Me very fine, eh? You think me pretty girl?"

"Owr. Vay pleh gel."

"Then that's that," said Twinkletoes, as she gathered her bargain tea-pot under her arm. "Good-bye, Serene Little Father Of Beautiful Children. Me see you to-night.

103

You hear me sing-dance."

"Yeh. Goo'pye!"

She flitted down the stairs. "Some pot! Won't the old man be pleased?"

In East India Dock Road she ran against a bandsman who had been dismissed from the Quayside for faulty time-keeping, the fundamental cause being the distance from the Blue Lantern to the Quayside.

" 'Ullo, flutey! Got the needle? You ain't looking gay."

"Don't feel gay, neither. Ain't 'ad one to-day."

"Well, let's take the glad road. Right here. Come on. I know you're up against it. 'Ave this with me."

They entered the Porcupine, and she bought him a Guinness.

"You sixteen?" asked the barmaid.

"Me? Rather. Turned sixteen."

"H'm. All right."

"You liar!" murmured the bandsman.

The bar was full of yellow boys, and,

104

depositing her tea-pot, Twinkletoes soon had a penny in the electric piano, which gurgled and throbbed an inviting melody. "'Ave a dance, old son!"

"No. Not here. Not among these toughs."

"They're all right." She turned and ogled the crowd deliciously, and made a grimace at her guest, which set him giggling in spite of himself. Then she held entreating arms to one of the yellow boys, and he came forward and allowed her to teach him intricate steps.

"'Ave 'nother, old son?" she cried to the bandsman as she waltzed.

"Righto. Guinness, please. 'Ere's fun!"

"'Appy days, old boy!"

When the piano ceased she returned to him. "Can't think how you can mix up with that gang. They're not—you know—something about 'em."

"Oh, they're all right. They're nice and kind. I don't care if they are batters, otherwise. I like batters. People don't bat unless they've some reason. Unless they've been through something. They can't get the best so they take the next best thing. And I don't blame 'em. We only live once. And there's one thing about 'em. They are alive. They wouldn't be batters if they weren't alive. It's only the dull old fools who can't feel nothing who don't bat. Go on—drink up and 'ave another. Like my new stockings?"

Back in Shantung Place she set the tea-pot proudly on the kitchen table where Dad would see it when he returned.

Then she went upstairs to the little bed-room. She lit a joss-stick which smouldered and filled the room with unnameable things of the East, and tenderly placed in the bottle a fresh bunch of violets. She knelt before them, with hands together, and prayed; not set prayers such as the religious ones pray, but the little thoughts that dared not lift their heads in the harsh world of necessity. Little hopes and fears and fancies which she

106

could not speak to living things would rise
in her heart and hover upon her lips in those
few moments when she communed with her
flowers; and it was as though she caught
from them something of their quality of
armored innocence. She could tell them
even the silliest things.

She told them what had happened to her
during the day. She asked them to be quick
and set old Mrs. Toplady right. She asked
them to contrive somehow to send the
Jenkins' kid to the seaside. She asked them
to stop old Garside's drinkings, and incident-
ally to let the horse that Garside had backed
come home on Saturday. She asked them
to bless old Dad, and Chuck Lightfoot, and
young Perce, and the girls she worked with;
and she begged them to help her to dance
better and to get a good "hand" that night.

Then she got up and stumped her toe
against the wash-stand and cried: "Suffering Jesus! What d'you do that for?" and
kicked the wash-stand sharply. She shed

107

frock and petticoat and stays, carefully combed and brushed her curls, and did a few spontaneous exercises with arms and legs. She stretched an impetuous leg taut in front of her.

"Some leg, Twinks!" she remarked appreciatively. It pleased her. She possessed very strongly the joy and pride of body; it was rapture for her to move her limbs. She gazed at it for a minute.

"Three pounds a week. And all out of a leg. Rum things—legs."

She washed legs and feet again and dressed, mumbling a cigarette. She shook a Chinese scent of pungent odor about her person, and looked for a coat. She chose the black velvet one, slipped into it, and threw her yellow tresses, which ran to her waist, outside it. The great envelope made her almost unbearably cuddleable, gave her the appeal of all young furred animals.

Downstairs she routed in a cupboard for a drop of Do-me-Good; she found only gin.

She sprawled on the sofa, and took a glass of it, and was then ready for her flying visit to the works.

.   .   .   .   .   .

Dad was laboring and swearing cheerfully in the Works when Chuck dropped in at about five o'clock.

"Ah. There y'are, old son. Come downstairs, will yeh? Want a word wi' yeh? Seen young Perce anywhere?"

"Nope."

" 'E ain't bin 'ere the last day or two. Thought 'e might be sick. I'll pop round t'night."

They went below, and Dad stroked his nose.

"Chuck—I'm thinking of finishing the down-stairs' biz."

"Eh?"

"Yerss. It's bin 'urting me for some time, now. All the time, reely. And I fancy it's getting a bit warm. The Prince

109

sent round t'other day for a special job, but I turned 'im down. I've done all right on this, but when it comes to big things I'm a False Alarm. Matter o' fac', I'm thinking of quitting at once."

"Well, now. . . . . No, but . . ."

"See, Chuck, y'know why I 'ad to take it on. But she's all right now. She's got a contract. And I'm through. She needn't never look back, now."

"Huh. And me?"

"Well, I dunno. You bin a good chap. 'Ere—why not quit, too? Why not go back? Why not run straight. I'm going to. Alwis thought you was a fool to drop Battling."

"I didn't. 'E dropped me. Drink."

"Wodyeh want to go on it for, at all? You didn't use to."

"Oh, you know all about it."

"Yerss. Funny 'ow she gets you that way, ain't it?"

"Um. I feel a fair shyster, going the

way I've gorn. But there ain't nothing else
fer me. I can't get back to the training
game. Battling wouldn't 'ave me nor no
one else. They don't trust me. I'm uncertain. You're all right. You got the biz
—the straight biz. But it ain't any use me
trying anything else. I got to keep on this
lay. I'm out."

"Great pity," said Dad sententiously.
"Great pity. Funny she got you that
way."

"Um. Well, there y'are. 'Taint no use
my trying. No one'd give me a chance. And,
as things were, there wasn't nothing for me
but the booze. You can't never know 'ow I
felt about 'er. Me, older and married. And
'er, so—so. . . . But there y'are. I've got
to stick it. Married to that blasted cow,
Cissie, too."

"Great pity. Wish I could do something."

"Oh, it don't matter, guv'nor. I'm out.
I can work other jobs on the same lay as this

111

one. There's plenty about who want stuff placed. . . ."

"Say—you won't ever let on, will yeh? Case it ever came round to 'er?"

"Blinkin' cats—wodyeh take me for?"

" 'Sall right, boy. On'y y'understand, now I'm going to run straight, 'ow nervy I feel. What'd she think o' me if she ever knew? When I think what she'd say and 'ow she'd look, it frightens me, Chuck. Fair frightens me. Alwis 'as. All the time I bin at it. Dunno 'ow I've lived through these yers. Playing a part, I bin. Playing up to 'er, and being gay and all that—letting 'er go on thinking I'm the straight feller she's alwis thought me. And the snide game at the back all the time."

"Trust me, guv'nor. I wouldn't do nothing that'd 'urt 'er ever so. See you at the Lantern, t'night. S'long."

VI

"CHUCK," said Dad at the Works a
few days later, "come round to-
night and 'ave a bit o' supper?
It's Twinks' birthday. Sixteen to-day. I'll
get the boys along. She'll be orf just after
eleven. She wants you to come."

Chuck looked wretched at the invitation,
but he accepted it. He had not the courage
to refuse; yet his heart sank at the prospect
of seeing Twinkletoes, as outrageously
happy as a street organ on a wet evening,
presiding as hostess at a table where he sat,
yet a thousand miles distant from him.

"Awright. I'll come along," he replied.

Dad had previously left instructions with
Twinkletoes to lay in a spread for her feast,
and to arrange for the boys.

"Get some sausages—or something that
cooks easy and looks nice. And you can
get some pease pudden to go with 'em round
at Abrahams'. And get some whisky for
the Prince. 'E don't touch beer. And some

wine for yesself. And 'ow about a little bottle o' Benedictine? We got a clean table-cloth, ain't we? And you can borrow some things from Mrs. Next-door if we ain't got everything. What about cheese? Better get some. And some fruit and biscuits. And don't be all day about it, neether. Mrs. Next-door'll give yer a hand. Get it all ready 'fore yeh go."

"Righto. You won't start 'fore I'm back, will yeh?"

"Wodyeh take us for, yeh little snorter? I 'ope we know manners. Start before the lady? The moment you puts yer nose round the door I'll 'ave the sausages into the pan and on the fire. See? And light the Annie-Maria in the front room 'fore yeh go."

"Good egg. But if I got to set all these things, what about it?"

"What about what?"

"Well, you'll 'ave to make a noise like money, that's all."

114

"Oh, well." He dug his hand in his pocket, and scattered a mass of silver over the table. "There y'are. And I 'ope we shall enjoy ourselves, bless yer little raspberry-tart."

He clasped her impulsively, and they danced an impromptu waltz.

"Good old pot," she cried, hitching a finger at her garter to straighten a creased stocking. "We'll set 'em alight. We'll daub the ruby on Shantung Place to-night. Who you asking?"

"Oh, the Prince and the Dook and one or two others."

"And Chuck?"

"Yes, I'll ask 'im."

"Yes, get Chuck along."

"And you'll bring oner two o' your gels, I s'pose?"

"I dessay."

"Then you better get some chocolates or sweets or something for 'em. Bye-bye."

Twinkletoes spent the morning in shop-
115

ping, and Mrs. Next-door in cleaning, so that
by evening the front room was ready for the
guests. The table was spread with a clean
cloth. A cluster of violets stood in a jam-
jar at the centre. A bright fire was burning
and on the plush-covered sideboard were
bottles that promised the uplifting of the
spirit. The front room was comfortable,
though furnished impulsively and with a
nice disregard for schemes. The piano, set
diagonally, occupied one corner. On the
floor in other corners were an accordion, a
mandolin, and tattered piles of music and
books. A couple of aspidistras were set in
the window. The mantelshelf and walls
were decorated with framed and unframed
photographs of Twinkletoes. Wherever you
looked you saw her: Twinkletoes as a toddler;
Twinkletoes in silk coat and lace hat;
Twinkletoes in her indoor frock and pina-
fore, reading; Twinkletoes in furs; Twinkletoes buried in brown velvet; Twinkletoes
robed only in a towel; Twinkletoes as a

116

pantomime fairy; Twinkletoes in an early Victorian ballet; Twinkletoes as Maud Allan; Twinkletoes in white silk and Scotch kilt; Twinkletoes as a winter spirit, as a summer spirit, as the voice of Spring, her slim body swathed only in ropes of roses; Twinkletoes in studies which still further accentuated her emphatic legs; and every one showing the essential Twinkletoes posed as for flight, resting on air. Even the cameras of Poplar could not ignore her urgent appeal. A few staid etchings—her own buying —hung here and there, though they were killed by reproductions of pictures of other little girls bought by Dad. He detested boys, but loved all little girls: each was to him a shadow of Twinkletoes.

At half-past eleven she arrived from the theatre with two of the Quayside girls. Dad opened the door to them, and bolted into the kitchen, leaving them to close it.

"I kep' me promise," he shouted. "I've got 'em on. 'Ear 'em sizzling?"

Twinkletoes sniffed voluptuously. "Smells good," she remarked, as they flung coats and hats on a chair in the passage. She swept into the front room, and found the gentlemen guests: The Pearly Prince, Dick the Duke, fat little Wallopy and Chuck Lightfoot, smoking cigarettes and talking discursively. They ended abruptly on two words from Chuck: "No shop, boys."

" 'Ullo, sweet children!" she cried. Then to the girls: "All the lads of the village." And again to the men: "Two of my rorty pals." She smiled amiably upon them. The Pearly Prince and Dick the Duke were uncles to her. They were, she understood, boxers, as indeed they were when nothing more lucrative presented itself. Wallopy she knew as a one-time shopkeeper who had been left a small annuity by a relative, and therefore was not compelled to do any regular work.

The Prince, who, at the moment they entered, was one of the Poplar boys, did his quick-change act and became the polished man of the West End bars. While the others remained seated, he rose. "Take my chair, kiddie," he said gracefully to the nearest of the girls, a maid of thirteen with vivid coloring and thick curls with the sheen of midnight water. "Quayside Kids, I think?"

"Yes," she answered, with a blush and a giggle. "And I know you. You're the Pearly Prince." She looked up at him in shy adoration. He received the worship gravely, but the sense of humor that had carried him through many tight corners awoke in a deprecatory twinkle in his eye.

"Ah," he said in a tone of paternal banter. "I'm just that. But I'm afraid I haven't got any pearls on me. If I had I'd put 'em round your pretty neck."

Little Wallopy inspected the two visitors. "Quaysides, eh? Ah, I useter dance when I was younger. But now——"

"Yes, now," said the slim Prince. "Now look at 'em. The Elephants' Gavotte. Five-

119

foot three, and sixteen stone if he's an ounce.
If you'd let me put you through it at the
medicine ball, now——"

"No good. Too sudden. No, I ought to
join the Quaysides. Three dances a night
among the babies'd get me down to normal,
I reckon. Think they'd take me on, kiddie?
I could do the Russian business all right.
Lift you up and swirl you round me shoulders—what?"

The two girls exploded into handkerchiefs,
and then Twinks and Dad entered with an
improbably huge dish of sausages, pease
pudding and mashed potatoes.

"You and Dad ought to go on together,
Wallopy," said Twinkletoes. "Simultane-
ous comedians. The Brothers Wallopy with
their Floppety Feet. There's money in it.
You'd be making a noise like a cash register
in no time."

"Now, come on," cried Dad. "Here's the
Aws Doov. Sit down, boys and gels, and
do things to 'em." They arranged them-
120

selves at the table while Wallopy took the bar under his control.

"Wine? Wine? Who's on wine?"

He planked a glass of Sauterne before the Prince's shy worshipper.

"There y'are, dear. Go on—smile for the pretty gentleman."

"Oh, don't, Mr—Mr——"

"I'm not mister. Do I look as if I were? 'Ow can an out-size in men like me be plain mister? I ask you! I'm Wallopy. Just Wallopy. Go on—say it after me: 'Thank you, Wallopy, for the assiduous manner in which you have catered to my wants in the matter of liquid refreshment.' Go on!"

"Thank you, Wallopy, for—— Oh, shut up, you silly old fool." And again she delivered a cascade of giggles.

"I see you 'smorning, Uncle Prince," cried Twinkletoes, poising a piece of sausage on a fork over which she ogled him. "I see you. I was on a tram, and I gave you a hooty one on two fingers. But you didn't get me. You

121

was going into the Lantern. Business, I
s'pose."

"Yes, it was business," said the Prince.

"Ah, I know that business." Wattlers and
Minesers. Seen 'em at it. Pease pudden,
Iris? Spuds? Shove 'em along, Chuck."

" 'Ow's the whisky, Pearly?" asked Dad.
"Top-hole."

"Ah, I thought you'd like it. A drop o'
special. Sammy travels in it, and 'e slipped
me a bottle."

"Well, get him to slip you a few more,
and I'll have 'em off you."

" 'Ow's the sausages, Wallopy?"

"The sausages," said Wallopy, threaten-
ing the giggling Iris with a dab of pease
pudding, "is all that sausages should be.
They're like me. Not much from the outside
but packed with good stuff inside."

"Well, we've made that dish look silly,
ain't we? 'Ave a bit o' cheese now. Come
on, Twinkle, stir yesself. Cheese."

When the cheese had disappeared the precious Benedictine was produced and shared among the men. Cigars, too, were produced for them, and a box of Turkish cigarettes for the girls.

Wallopy's smooth lines expressed admiration. "Cigars. Benny. Turkish cigarettes. Lor, we can go it, cant we? Wish I'd got married and 'ad a kid on the stage. Cigars and Benny. Just by 'opping about and keeping time with the band."

"Um," said Twinkletoes. "I'm glad I was born with a leg, if only to provide you with a Benny and cigars. The new liquor—*Crême de la Leg*. When you drink that Benny, you must drink to my legs. It's all a matter of legs, ain't it, kids? When my legs begin to go, then there'll be an end of good things. All comes down to legs. Faces ain't no good. Look at Iris—awfully jolly to look at when she's undressed, but her nose ain't right. It's crooked. But if you're talking of legs . . . You 'ave a look at 'ers when she gets up."

123

"Shut up, Twinks!" spluttered Iris, her face burning with discomfiture at this dissection of her person before the aloof Prince; for where Twinkletoes was fearlessly innocent she was shamefully innocent.

"Well," said Dad, "I felt we oughter push a boat out on an occasion like this. 'Tain't every day that the leader of the Quayside Kids 'as a birthday. 'Tain't every day that Twinkletoes is sixteen."

"That's so," said Wallopy, as he clambered up. "Now, boys and gels, a toast. Twinkletoes is sixteen. 'Ere's wishing 'er all she wishes 'erself, and if she's as sweet and as happy and as prosperous at sixty as she is at sixteen, she won't 'ave nothing to grumble about, eh? From the start she's made, we expect great things of her, and when she's got on and gorn to West End theatres, with photos in all the papers, and a motor car and a country 'ouse and diamonds and what-not, and forgotten all about 'er old friends down 'ere, we shall still be proud to know that we

124

knew 'er when she was starting, and that we drank to her—*and* 'er legs. Boys—I give you Twinkletoes and 'er legs."

The company rose; and five of London's smartest lower-grade criminals solemnly and sincerely drank to the health and success of the beautiful child of their colleague.

Twinkletoes giggled and kicked her legs in response.

"That was a milky one!" she cried, finding no suitable words to express what she felt. She loved these friends of her Dad's. The warm glow of their humanity and good-fellowship had enriched her little life during the last four years, and she had revelled in them. The Pearly Prince was the high example of courtesy. Wallopy was a fat old thing with whom you could do and to whom you could say what you liked. Dick the Duke was a taciturn, rather somber individual, but lit with gleams of humor; and whenever Twinkletoes desired to flutter a half-crown on a horse, it was to Dick that she would go, and he always gave her something that came home.

"Come on, creatures," she said, rising impulsively, "let's get these things out and be comfortable."

Dad and the three girls cleared the dishes and table to the kitchen; and while the men smoked and sipped their drinks Twinkletoes took her mandolin, fluttering with radiant ribbons, and sat on the sofa with her companions and made music for the light voice of Iris. She played idly, mechanically, but Iris, though keeping her eyes from the Pearly Prince, sang always to him; and she went through all the bubbly, colored melodies that she knew: *Dolce Napoli, Santa Lucia, O sole Mio, Monaco, Funiculi-Funicula, Sur les Ponts de Paris* and *Siciliana*.

For an hour they held talk and song; then the Pearly Prince rose. "Well, better be making a move, I suppose. Had a jolly time, Minasi, thanks."

"Oh, glad you've enjoyed yesself."

"Not going?" asked Twinkletoes.

"Must. Quite time."

"Well, have another 'fore you go?"

"No, I won't have another. I got to see a man of business at my rooms. About that fight next week."

"Oh, go on. One won't hurt you. 'Ave a short snort with a sport. Else I shall play rough-house with you."

"No, thanks."

"Iris—you ask him."

"Do have one, Mr. Prince."

"Oh, all right. You're great kids. I'll have one to your bright eyes. And Twinkletoes' legs. And I hope I shall be invited to your next birthday-party."

"Oh sure. And it'll be Champagne next year, I hope. You never know. If they want to renew my contract, I shall stick the price up."

"Good. If I were young and silly enough I'd marry you or Iris. But, thank God, I got more sense."

"Come on, Twinks," said Dad. "Get yer 'at and coat. We better see the kids 'ome. It's getting late. 'Tany rate we'll see 'em on their way."

They went out with much festive clatter, and parted with Wallopy, the Duke and the Prince at the corner, after prolonged crying of farewells, remembrances, appreciations of the evening and "Don't be late in the morning!"

The girls were left at their respective streets, and Dad and Twinkletoes were returning to Shantung Place when they saw a black fester of people at the gates of the Galloping Horses.

Now Dad, being a man of simple tastes, was always drawn by the divine simplicity of a street fight. It acted on him as a red rag on a bull. At such a spectacle his eyes would light, his nostrils quiver and his feet dance a double-shuffle, until, unable longer to remain neutral, he would charge in and lend a hand to whichever party in the dispute seemed to be getting the more punishment. In two shakes of a guinea-pig's tail—as he would have figured it—he was across the road with Twinkletoes in pursuit.

The night of East India Dock Road does not die on the twelfth stroke of the clock. The doors of the taverns may be bolted and barred; the clanging gates of the corner hotels may be hurled into their sockets at that hour; but the night laps well over the morning to the extent of two and sometimes three hours, and often its mournful echoes will disturb the dawn. Impromptu concerts are given; insults grow precociously to blows; impromptu vows of eternal comradeship are sworn; and life-long friendships are shattered in a space of moments.

From the heart of the crowd came a lone cry in those accents that carry the wail of Western Ireland:

"Arr now, but he called me wife a porker."

"No, but 'e's 'pologised," protested the crowd.

The Man of Seven Sorrows and the wailing voice was invisible, but it was evident from his articulation that he was engaged in a physical contest.

"Lemme be, will ye now, lemme be! Lemme get to him."

" 'Old 'im back, there!"

"We can't 'old 'im back no longer."

The loungers parted in a panic, their feet chattering along the pavement as the struggler broke loose from the restraining arms. Old Dad, worming his way to the front, obtained a clear view of the contestants: an outraged Irishman and a little scraggy man who was too patently drunk to be worth fighting. A dented bowler hat was riding on his left ear. He swayed. He looked always at the Irishman, and seemed struggling to repress a smile. But apparently the thought of the physical proportions of the other chap's wife was too appealing to be resisted.

"Porker!" he murmured, and figured the

word to the crowd with extended arms as of one embracing a barrel.

The husband was alert, sober and angry. His friends had drawn away from him. It was useless to hold him back. Their faces carried the weariness and despair of those who have failed where they expected to fail.

The drunk, finding himself popular, fixed a banana skin in his buttonhole. "Ta' 'ome to missus," he explained. He essayed a graceful dance. He asked his audience how, while not wishing to be offensive, anyone could describe old Flanagan's wife as other than a por——

Then he sat suddenly down, and Twinkletoes, peering under shoulders and through chinks in the crowd, had great joy of her glimpses of the comedy.

From one of the lurking alleys came a cold, insistent voice. The drunk heard it. Thoughtfully he began to unlace his boots. Through the chuckling audience came a strenuous figure, hatless. She gathered her intoxicated man by the collar and shook him.

The aggrieved husband moved forward. "That's right," he said; "take him away. He's bin insulting me wife, he has, and he can think himself lucky I didn't do things to him. But I didn't. 'Cos he's drunk. Quite drunk."

Then the comedy took a new turn. At the word "drunk" the little man broke from his wife's clutch. His lips parted for speech, but none came. He looked around to discover the slanderer. He saw the Irishman standing before him. He staggered forward and struck him forcefully on the mouth with his fist. The astonished victim stepped back. He put his hand to his mouth.

"Ah, now, ye will have it for that!" And they closed.

"Separate 'em! Separate 'em!" cried those on the outer ring, crying with the more vigor since their position ruled them out as possible volunteers. Many windows creaked and opened. Through them were thrust heads towzled with the pillow but alight with interest. The men swayed and slithered and swung. When the wife of the drunk sailed in to hamper her husband's burly opponent she was put out by an elbow in the breast. She staggered with it to the crowd, which echoed her gasp in little ripples. A lamp on an opposite corner threw a half-hearted illumination. Here and there a cigarette glowed like an evil eye.

"Why don' someone separate 'em?"

"Who's got a whistle?"

"See that? Right on the nose. Look— 'e's biting 'is 'and."

A woman wailed. "Stop 'em, cancher? Call yesselves men? They're killing one another. Eu! 'E's banging 'is 'ead on the pavement. Eu! I can't look."

Dad moistened his hands. He looked round for Twinkletoes. Said Dad: "Your little pot-and-pan is about fed up on this.

133

You stop 'ere, old Gawd-forbid, and don't you dare move. Out of the way, there!"

He lifted up his voice, and it was a voice worth lifting. At the very sound of his roared command those in front dropped back. "Stan' away, I tell yeh!"

He was inside the ring. His sympathies went at once to the drunk, and it was at the Irishman's collar that he sprang. He got an arm-lock, and drew his man steadily back. "Someone keep the little 'un off," he commanded. Two or three made a dash and secured the little 'un.

Then the fight ended. The banana skin, hanging loosely from the little 'un's buttonhole, dropped to the ground. Straining backward, Dad dug his heels into the wooden roadway for a purchase. At the third step he struck the banana skin, slipped, and fell, and remained prone and motionless, eyes closed.

Twinkletoes gave a little scream and rolled her hands in her frock. She tried to get to

134

Dad, but the crowd was winding into itself. Oh, Dad! He was hurt—perhaps killed. And this was her birthday. Why had she let him do it? Why hadn't she pulled him away?

The audience hummed. Women gave little gasps and turned away. Those at the back, who could not see, said: "Police!" "Doctor!" Those nearest, after a satisfying stare, turned away, or approached fearfully and retreated fearfully. A woman's voice from an upper window cried: "Whassup?" and this gave an opportunity to some to escape decently. They went to her. Five different voices grated harshly on the night, crying five different versions. She was a strong woman, but, being half asleep, she made no attempt to follow the plots of five involved romances, and the window went down with the rickety rattle.

"Well, that's all over," said the usual philosopher. " 'E's gorn. Standing and staring won't bring 'im back, will it? But 'e's a blasted 'ero. That's what 'e is. And a damn fool."

The two opponents forgot their quarrel. The drunk grabbed his wife's arm, the Irishman took his other arm, and they disappeared in amity, all differences wiped out by the new tragedy.

At last the crowd had thinned sufficiently to enable Twinkletoes to wriggle through. She dashed into the ring towards the prostrate and lifeless Dad, but, as she pounced upon him, he made one swift movement and was on his feet. He shook himself and looked with a grin at Twinkletoes, white, trembling and fearful.

"That's that," he said.

"Oh, Dad, I thought you was 'urt. I thought you was killed."

"Me 'urt? Garn. Take a lot o' that to 'urt me."

"Then you're all right?"

"Absolutely."

Her face broke into ripples of laughter as

136

he toddled away at her side. "I done it apurpose," he went on. "Y'see, they was getting bad-tempered like, and might do one another a injury. And I couldn't 'ave 'eld that Irish bloke back fer long. So when I slipped I thought I'd stay down an' give 'em a shock. Soon's anyone's 'urt, y'know, a fight alwis stops. You'll notice that."

Twinkletoes gurgled and looked up at him. "Oo, Dad. I've alwis said you was wonderful, and blimey, you are. You're the fair top-liner. Oo, I am glad. I made sure you was 'urt. . . . What a birthday! Your present was good, and the supper was fine, and the boys were all jolly; but this little crush 'as put the lid on everything. Grand finale with augmented orchestra. I believe you arranged it specially, 'cos it was my birthday. Did you?"

Dad chuckled non-committally.

"You reely are a marvellous old man."

"Well, kid, I on'y 'ope every other birthday'll be as jolly, and that you'll enjoy 'em when you're seventy as much as you 'ave this one."

"Me too. Oo—ain't people and things *lovely!*"

VII

THE Blue Lantern bar was happy: all its friends were there—that little band of pilgrims that lived in the East and worshipped in the West. Its doors flapped back and forth, emitting great gasps of festal noise. The Pearly Prince was there, tall and vibrant, resplendent in blue serge. Dick the Duke was there, in a suit of noisy grey, with rings and chains about his person. Little Wallopy was there, in a fawn coat and Robin Redbreast waistcoat, and Chuck Lightfoot, quiet and neat, a muffler about his throat. The indecently ragged Hank crouched in his accustomed corner.

When Divisional Detective-Inspector Territon entered in mufti, with an air of careful detachment, he was greeted with noncommittal nods.

"Wanting me?" asked the Prince.

"Not yet, me boy. But I'll plant a few commas in your story 'fore long, if not a full stop."

"Ah, we'll see about that."

Territon ordered a beer and placed himself next Hank Hogan.

"Well, how's things, Hank?" he asked, with superior familiarity.

"Oh, mustn't grumble."

"Have one?"

"I don' mind. Same again."

Dickery-Dock came forward with elephantine obsequiousness at sight of Territon and served the drinks. He and the crowd looked askance at one another, speculating as to the cause of this visit.

"Went up to the Quayside," Territon volunteered, "last night. T'see that kid of Minasi's. Twinkletoes, don't they call her?"

"Ar."

"Fine kid. Wonderful kid. Minasi's a great chap too."

"Ar."

"Great chap. How's he doing now? Doing well, ain't he?"

"I dunno. I see 'im in 'ere sometimes."

140

"He ought to be doing well. What with the business and what that kid of his makes. She's a marvel. Fair marvel. What'd you reckon he makes?"

"Couldn't tell yeh. I know I ain't making anything. If it wasn't for me Old Age Pension I'd be in a fair old mess-up."

"M'm. Pity. But you've had a good run, eh?"

"Ar."

"Will Minasi be in here to-night? I want to see him rather special."

"Dunno."

Territon inspected Hank, and Hank received the scrutiny without a flicker. "Hank," he said at length, "you know everything what goes on. Do you know anything about his die-stamping business?"

"Nothing."

"Have you ever wondered why he does so well?"

" 'Tain't none of my biz to wonder about other people's. I'm wondering about me own."

141

"Well, I tell you straight. I got the wire about him yesterday. I've had the office. Never mind how. Now where I'm a bit uncertain——" He paused, fearing he had said too much.

Hank said "Ar" impressively. "Seems to me," he went on, "that yer wasting yer beer and yer time. What th'ell d'yeh think I know about Minasi? I ain't a blasted nark, am I?"

"No, but . . . I like Minasi. And I thought you might have heard."

Hank's face took the tinge of his hair. His voice rose to an indignant squeak. "An' if I 'ad? Eh! An' if I 'ad? If you want a blasted nark, don't come to me, guv'nor. See? Don't come to me. If yeh wants lies, I'll tell yeh plenty. A dozen t'every 'alf-pint. But that's all I can tell yeh about Minasi. 'Cos I don't know nothing. See?" He turned his back on him and impolitely ignored him.

Territon grinned ruefully, yet appreciatively. "You're a deep 'un, Hank. Deep as they make 'em. I suppose I sha'n't never get you. But I got Minasi all right. Any time now. And I'll have the Prince and the Dook 'fore they're much older. I give yeh *my* word. I'll hand them theirs, sure enough."

He drank up and went away, followed by contemptuous stares.

"Every time I see that bloke," said the Pearly Prince, "I get the fidgets in me boot. Some day I sha'n't be able to resist it."

"Old 'Ank told 'im orf all right," said the Duke. "What was 'e on, 'Ank?"

"Oh, I d'no. Some guff about a girl— one of the hop-joint girls and flapdoodle of that sort."

"Oh. Thought it might 'ave been on our lay."

"Oh no," said Hank. "No."

Hank had gained high reputation in the Lantern district where reputations are achieved with difficulty. He was held to be as moral as a tom-cat, the pink of impropriety. He carefully nourished this legend of an oblique career; it brought drinks; and he went about crying through his manner: "I'm a bad man, that's what I am. I'm a bad man." Only he and a few chosen friends knew that the legend was spurious. He had done nothing more daring than a little pocket-picking in his youth. He was one of the sweetest, kindest and most faithful of comrades: the confidant of the district. His headquarters was the Lantern, and thither men would go when troubles beset them.

Far behind him was a story. In his youth he had met a girl connected with one of the thousand religious missions that infest the Limehouse ways. He developed a passion for the Word, but his yearning for the intangible glories of the life to come had its foundation in something very near to this world. He worshipped this mission-girl; and she, finding that he only attended meetings when she was there, and only listened

144

to the Word as preached or sung by herself,
came regularly to preach and to sing and to
expound privately to him the mysteries and
wonders of the faith she held. To her he
listened. He sat at her feet and believed
everything, simply because she said that it
was so. About the streets he would follow
her, never approaching within uncomfortable
distance, but hanging, as it were, about her,
that he might, if ever the need arose, be there
to succor her.

When she was prevented, by slight illness
or other preoccupation, from attending the
mission, he returned to the Lantern; and
she quickly saw that if one soul had been
snatched from the pestilence, it was she and
she alone who could retain it.

One night, when she had been absent from
three meetings, she met him staggering from
the Lantern; and she stopped him, and gave
him a look such as he had never seen on any
face before. Late that night he went to her,
at the headquarters of the Crusade, and he

knelt at her feet in misery, and prayed for-
giveness, touching with shy finger-tips her
proffered hand, and kissing the border of her
skirt.

Then she found that, having given so much
of herself, she must give more. She found
that, like all humans, she was more drawn to
love someone she had helped than someone
who had helped her. The beautifying of his
heart was her work; without her it would
again become dulled and tarnished. So when
he next came to her, humble and tragic and
ridiculous, she married him.

He reached his heaven. He went away
from the mission hall rapturously forswear-
ing all the dear old dirty days. Away went
the lamp and the pipe, away went the bottle
and the glass, and contemptuous feet
stamped splendidly away from such places
as the Lantern. For a year he remained with
his Jesus woman in paradise. Then a child
was born. The child was born dead; the
mother died three days later.

146

He tore up Bible and Prayer Book, and smashed the harmonium with a hatchet. And he flung through the doors of the Lantern, which snapped happily behind him, and hammered on the bar, shouting: "Double gin! Double gin! And bloody quick about it. Yers since I 'ad one."

Later, he rolled out and crawled to the cottage now empty of delight; and as he had gone home that night so he went home every night that followed.

When he had inverted his tankard, he looked at Chuck. Chuck came across and had it replenished.

"Well, lad, 'ow is it?"

"Oh, fair," said Chuck.

"You're looking better. Does it 'urt as much?"

"Oh, hell. Don't ask."

"Ar. . . . By the way, that wasn't 'alf a doing you gave young Perce."

"Oh. You 'ear about it.

"Ar."

147

"Course, you 'ear everything."

"Yerss. I 'eard about it. I 'ear a lot, as you say. Everything, nearly. Chuck, Territon wasn't 'ere for nothing to-night."

"No?"

"No. Chuck, take a 'oliday."

"Whaffor?"

"Take a 'oliday. And Minasi too. Both of yeh."

"Whaffor?"

"Don't keep saying 'Whaffor.' Know me, don't yeh? Well, then, I says: Take a 'oliday. And I says Territon, too. And I says Snide. Where's Minasi?"

"Down at the Works, I think."

"Ar. Well, you better go down there. Quick. And see 'im. Don't talk too much. The Prince and the Dook and Wallopy can fix their lie-up all right. But go and see Minasi. And just say to him what I told yeh. 'Olidays. Territon. Snide."

"Hank, you're smart. I didn't get you at first. What chance we got?"

"Any amount. 'E don't know nothing. 'E's on'y guessing. Tried to suck me. E'll be using me for a rubber stamp next."

Chuck became suddenly emphatic:

"Christ. If it should get about. If it was to come off. If Twinkletoes—— My God! *I* don't mind. I'll take what's coming to me. But if she—— Christ. 'Sall right, though. I'll fix that, some'ow. Whatever 'appens, she'll never 'ear of it. There's plenty of ways. I'll slip along to the Works. S'long."

VIII

TO Twinkletoes in the dressing-room of the Quayside came the girl Lilac. She stood over Twinkletoes' chair, one shoulder listed scornfully.

"Huh!" she grunted.

"What's the matter?"

"Huh! 'My Dad's one of the finest men in the world. My Dad's clean all through. My Dad's never done anything dirty. My Dad's the straightest man that ever lived.' Huh!"

"What you talking about?"

"You and your glorious, marvelous old Dad."

Twinkletoes turned upon Lilac, a little spark of anger appearing in her eyes, as it always did when anyone ridiculed or aspersed the old Dad. "Well, what about it?" She noticed that the other girls were watching and grinning mischievously. Their happy faces were deformed by a mixture of spite and amusement.

"Cuh! Your Dad never done anything dirty!"

"Lilac, what d'you mean? Talking like that. Nor 'e 'asn't. What's up with you?"

"Stow it, Twinks. Don't make out you don't know. Everybody knows about it. I heard it 'smorning. We all know about it."

Twinkletoes stood up. Her face was alabaster. Her lips were twisted. "Know about what?"

"Why, about your Dad. About his tricks. What he is."

"Tricks? Tricks? Lilac—you trying to make a row?"

"Don't be silly, Twinks. No. Only don't go swanking any more. Because we know. We like you, Twinks, awfully, but we can't stand your swank about your Dad. Not any more. Seeing what your Dad is and has been for years."

"Oh. And what is he?" She trembled a little.

"Why, everybody knows what he is. He's

151

a forger. He makes bad notes at these Works of his. And he's going to be locked up soon."

Twinkletoes dropped back to the ledge which served as dressing-table. Her hands gripped its edge. She stared at Lilac. Exploding giggles drew her eyes to the other girls. She looked from one to the other, then back to Lilac. Her breath came awkwardly. Three times she opened her mouth to speak, but said nothing. She seemed as one suffering strangulation. This was, she argued, a joke. Should she take it as a joke, or regard it as an insulting joke? Or was it a deliberate and arranged assault on her leadership? She decided to treat it cursorily.

"Don't be a fool, Lilac. You'll get yesself into trouble some day—spreading lies about people like that."

A scream of laughter followed the remark. She looked round, first, threateningly; then smiled in an effort to placate them.

152

"Look 'ere—what's all this about? Who put this up? If you can't think of a better guff that this, try again."

Lilac seemed a little abashed. She glanced at her companions.

"Twinks—do you honestly mean to stand there and tell us you don't know?"

"Of course I don't know rubbish like that —silly."

Lilac, in petticoat and stockings, thrust her head earnestly forward and clasped her hands. She was very serious.

"Twinkletoes—it's *true*! True as I stand here. True as God's in heaven. Everybody knows it."

"Yes," shrieked the children, "we all know it. Your Dad's a forger! Your Dad's a forger!" they chanted to an impromptu air. The younger ones joined hands and danced round her. "Your Dad's a forger! Your Dad's a for—ger! He'll be locked up in pri—son! He'll be locked up in pri—son!" while Lilac cried: "Stop it, kids! Shut up!"

153

Slowly, very slowly, Twinkletoes realized that something had happened. Her eyes bulged. Her head drooped. The separate golden curls were mournfully pendulous. Then her temper reached its flash-point. She sprang away from the dressing-slab.

"Liars! Liars! Liars!" she screamed. "Liars—the whole lot of you! Suffering Jesus, I'll smash you for that. I'll smash you!"

A chair fell with a mild thud as she thrust an arm full at the concerned face of Lilac. A hair-brush spun into the grinning group. Shoes and boots went at them. She became maniac: a livid little creature bent on destroying these foul things that had touched with their dirty tongues her splendid Dad. The youngest drew back, afraid not so much of her blows as of this storm that they had aroused. She swept across the floor after them, pummelling here, tearing there, shaking others, throwing the whole weight and fire of her body into this righteous crusade.

154

Only when Lilac and two of the biggest girls had gripped her and thrown her to the ground did the fury cease. She lay limp, sobbing dry sobs.

"Cads! Cads! Cads!" she gasped. "If my Dad was here. . . . Liars! Cads! Lemme get up."

Lilac, shamefaced, helped her up.

"Twinks—don't be so silly. It *is* true. Ask anybody. Ask Hank Hogan, that old beast that's always in the Blue Lantern. Ask Mrs. Lightfoot—her husband works for your Dad and gets the notes round. Ask Roseleaf. Ask Inspector Territon. He lives in our street, and told my Dad. They're all going to be arrested. Ask anybody. Everybody knows.

"We're all sorry, Twinks dear, but we thought you knew, and we got wild because you were always talking that way. We thought it was swank. It isn't your fault. We're not blaming you. You'll always be the same to us, whatever happens.

155

"Here—come on—quick, or you won't be ready to go on."

Twinkletoes suffered herself to be led to her chair, and sat staring into the mirror at the curious figure who used to be Twinkletoes, and now was . . .? They were so serious about it. Yet it must be wrong. There was a mistake. Her Dad—her old pot-and-pan—doing things like that. It wasn't possible. Things didn't happen like that. It was surely some other man they'd got mixed up about. But they were so certain. The pulses hammered into her brain one sing-song phrase: *Suppose it's true! Suppose it's true!* "Everybody knows. . . . Ask Hank Hogan. . . . Ask Inspector Territon. . . . Ask Mrs. Lightfoot."

The Ma of the troupe bustled in. "All ready, girls? Now then, Minasi, hurry up. You're always late. Hurry up, I said. What's the matter?"

The girls stood around in a disturbed bunch.

156

"It's her father, Ma."

"Well, what about 'im?"

"He's going to be locked up."

"Well, well, and if 'e is. 'E's not the only one that's been locked up. Come, Minasi. It's a bit awkward like, but there's no need to make all this fuss."

"Oh, lemme alone. Lemme alone!" she wailed. "I wish I was dead. I wish—— Oh, it ain't true. It can't be. I'm going to see."

"Minasi—you stop here." But in a streak of brown she was gone through the door and down the stairs.

Her first thought was to go to Dad, but that, she felt, was impossible. If it wasn't true, it would be a dirty thing to let him think she even allowed the story to worry her for a moment. If it were true, it would be too horrible to see him. As she ran, she mumbled: "Oh, Dad, Dad!"

She thought of Chuck Lightfoot, of Inspector Territon, of Hank Hogan. She

157

fixed on Hank. She knew him; he had been sometimes to the house, and, although he was dirty, he was always nice and kind. On the corner where stands the Blue Lantern she found him. Funds had run out; the Lantern bar was empty; and he was searching the streetscape with his keen eyes for a friend who should be safe for "one."

Hatless, panting, dishevelled, she stumbled against him.

"Oh, 'Ank, 'Ank, it ain't true, is it? What everybody's saying 'bout my Dad?"

Hank started momentarily, then chewed steadily on his quid of plug. " 'Bout yer Dad? Why, Twinks, whassup? Knocking a por old man down like that. What ain't true?"

"What they're saying!"

"What're they saying? I can't answer 'alf-a-dozen questions at once with all the breath knocked out o' me. One at a time, and put 'em plainly." But his face was troubled. The fury of her questions perplexed him. His manner expressed a desire to find some means of getting rid of Twinkletoes. For the first time in his life he found that being a fount of local information was a nuisance.

" 'Bout Dad forging notes. And going to be locked up. Oh, it ain't true?"

Hank looked up the street; then at Twinkletoes. He became at once shy and awkwardly demonstrative.

"Why, there now, fancy asking me a thing like that. 'Ow d'you think I sh'd know?"

"Oh, don't. You do know. You know everything 'bout these things. They said Inspector Territon told someone 'e was going to arrest Dad 'fore long. What d'you know, 'Ank? Tell me. Tell me."

"Why—can't say I know nothing 'bout it. Best man fer you t'ask is—is—yer Dad. Or Territon. Or someone who's in it. I couldn't tell yeh." He looked away. "Ar —there's a pal o' mine over there I want to see partic'lar." He pulled his coat about him. "I'll pop across, kiddie. So long."

" *'Ank!*"

He turned and looked down at her. He noted the dumb agony in her face, and his wild red hair, filthy clothes and tender manner gave him the appearance of a caricatured angel pronouncing a benediction. He placed a hand on her shoulder, and lifted one of the curls. "Brace up, kiddie." He slid across the road, and she knew from what she had seen in his face that it was true.

Her god had fallen.

With sick, faltering steps she moved away, going, for no reason, back to the Quayside, moaning "Dad!" at every pace. In the stage door passage she met Markie Roseleaf. He stood away from her, his hands in the pockets of his greasy dress suit, the stricken animal moving even a theatrical manager to silence and wonderment.

"Por kid," he said, with insufferable kindness. "Por kid," and stopped her as she blundered to the stairs. " 'Sall right, kid.

160

You needn't work to-night. They're nearly on. I know all about it. Por li'l gel. Ain't there nothing we can do?"

"No. No. I don' want nothing."

"I'm so sorry. We all are. All of us. Honest, we are. Really. No codding. 'Ere, brace up, kiddie. Look up. Wish I could do something for yeh." He seemed at a loss. "It give me a bit of a jar when it was told me. Never suspected it. Known yer old Dad fer years and—never dreamt of anything like this. Never dreamt of it. There —run up and see the gels, when they're orf. They're sorry they chipped you. Told me so. All of 'em. 'Orrible busines. Specially for fine kid like you. Awfully sorry. I am, reely."

Twinkletoes lagged up the stairs to the Kids' dressing-room, and fell into her chair. She rested her arms on the slab and drooped. Her little body shook with sharp, cold sobs. No tears came: only a sickness inside that seemed to tear and gnaw her.

161

When the kids were off they came upstairs quietly, not in the usual pell-mell scramble. So swift, so complete was the metamorphosis from the joyous, blasphemous, adorable child who had led them, into the white, whipped, soulless bundle before them that they were hushed in her presence.

Lilac, very penitent, touched her shoulder.

"Twinks, Twinks—forgive us. We're all sorry. We didn't know the way you felt about it. Will you forgive us?"

"Oh, 'sall right. It don' matter. I don' mind 'bout that."

"You forgive us, then?"

"Um."

"Twinks, don't brood like that. Don't take it that way. You'll be ill. Twinks—lift up."

"Oh, don't, don't," she moaned. "Lemme alone." She shook herself.

"No, Twinks. Twinks dear, don't go on like this."

Anomalous noises came from the buried

162

face. She writhed as one eluding flames or blades.

"Oh, God. Oh, Dad. Oh, go 'way."

Then, with a rush of hideous sobs, the tears came, bitter tears and full sobs that seemed to scorch the eyes and wrench the small throat. She was no longer a little girl, but a tortured organism.

The others, neglecting washing and changing, stood back, uncertain whether the final outburst meant a fainting fit or the last paroxysm before death. The younger ones watched, morbidly fascinated by the spectacle of abandoned agony. Some suggested fetching Ma. Others were for fetching Roseleaf. One or two wanted a doctor.

But Lilac went to her, lifted her from the slab, wound entreating arms about her, and pillowed her on her shoulder. There she finished her fight, the measure of her tears growing gradually less with the sobs, until, after a long space, she was tranquil, save for spasmodic coughs.

163

"Feel better, Twinks?"

"Um."

"That's right. You've had a cry. Now you want to be cheered up. It's no use moping. It won't help things. You'll have to keep as bright's you can. We'll all help. Won't we?"

"Yes. Any way we can. Not 'alf!"

"Thanks."

·Lilac rocked her in her arms. "What you want to do now? Going home?"

"Oh, I dunno. No. I can't go 'ome. I can't go 'ome. No. Oh, Lilac!"

"There, kid. No, it won't be much use your going 'ome. You won't sleep. I know you won't. You'll only get mopey and broody by yourself."

Twinks raised herself a little. "You going with the crowd to-night, Lilac?"

"Well, we did think of going, but——"

"I'll come wi' you."

Lilac pondered. "Yes," she said at length; "would be better, perhaps. Best thing you

164

could do, come to think of it. Might cheer you up a bit. You want something rackety. Take you out of yourself like."

"Where you going?"

"Oh, the Lantern. Downstairs. Me and one or two others, and some of the boys, and Freddie Parslow. Quite private it'll be. Just ourselves. I think it'll do you good, really."

"I want to die, Lilac."

"Oh, don't, Twinks. No good talking like that. I know how you feel, ducksie. But it won't do. It won't help matters."

Twinkletoes threw herself from Lilac's arms, and became suddenly alive. She jumped up. "All right. I'll come. I don't care *where* I go to-night. I'll come any-where. Get ready."

"That's right," said Lilac, turning to the crowd with a touch of pride in her manner as though to say: "There! We didn't want a doctor. I've done her good!"

At the stage door was Roseleaf. " 'Ullo, kiddie. Coming along with us. That's the style. Lilac'll look after you. We'll try to cheer you up a bit. Whatever's 'appened don't make no diffs to us."

She followed them with a desperate gaiety. Her god had fallen. She would celebrate the fall with fitting rites.

They reached the Blue Lantern and by a private door descended to the basement saloon, reserved for various obscure "clubs" and societies. It was brightly lit, and set with tables and crimson plush lounges. An open piano stood in a corner, its top covered with wine, beer and spirit bottles, with corks drawn. Sandwiches were on a small green-baize table. A lounge in the corner, built in decks like a ship's berths, was for the use of those who liked the lamp. The odor was sickly; the air dry. Cheap sporting prints disfigured the walls.

The company included Roseleaf; the two comedians of that week's show; Twinkletoes, Lilac, and three others of the older girls of the troupe, between sixteen and seventeen;

166

the conductor of the Quayside; the electrician; the electrician's wife, and one or two of the bandsmen.

Roseleaf called for Dickery-Dock with magnanimous geniality, and the bottles were served. The girls took wine. The electrician's wife took gin and water. The others chose whisky or beer.

"Come on, Lilac," said Roseleaf proprietorially. "Get busy. Show us 'ow it's done. And put some ginger into it. We want warming up to-night."

"All right, guv'nor." Lilac moved obediently to the piano. She loved these forbidden underground escapades. They were life to her: adventure; something different from the poor round of her work on the halls and her mornings in the stuffy rooms of her home with quarrelsome parents. She was at that age when she was tired of ordinary things; an age of wanting something to happen; of wanting you know not what: chiefly, perhaps, of wanting to want

167

something. Nothing happened in her life.
She did the same things every day; met the
same people; performed the same tasks; and
they fed her up. These little excursions
after the show with Roseleaf opened the
ivory gate to her, and gave her palate just
that salted flick that it needed. In these
affairs she could live; she could let herself
go.

She strummed idly on the piano for a
space; then, with a crash of chords her young
hands and bare arms flashed along the keys
in a provocative rag-time that stung the
blood and set muscles moving against their
will, and immediately the room seemed to
blaze with carnival lights.

Twinkletoes, pale and dried as a statue,
sat staring before her, wondering whether
she had ever been the Twinkletoes of yesterday. She had no interest in anything.
There was no hope for her of entertainment.
She was there because she was not elsewhere.
She hardly knew she was there. Her body

168

was reclining on a lounge, but mind and soul were suspended. White wine was placed before her, and she gulped it, and lit a Turkish cigarette.

All were smoking, and through the entwining haze she saw Roseleaf cross to Lilac at the piano, move her straight, short hair that reached just to her collar, and put his lips to the back of her neck. Yesterday she wouldn't have liked it, but it didn't matter now.

"Go way, guv'nor," laughed Lilac skittishly, twisting nimbly but not ceasing her melody. "Go 'way. I'll beat you."

"Try it" he chuckled. He held a glass of wine to her mouth, and she lapped it while keeping the intricate beats of the rag. He gave her a word, and she played a yearning melody to which he sang, inviting the company to join in the chorus. Nine voices roared it:

We sha'n't 'ave no Wore
As long's we 'ave a King like good King Edward,
There won't be no Wore

169

'Cos 'e 'ates that koind of thing—guh!
We sha'n't 'ave no Wore
  As long's we 'ave a King like good King Edward
   Peace with 'Onner
   Is 'is Motter
   Gawd save—
        the King—guh!

Roseleaf strolled idly round. Coming before Twinkletoes, he looked down at her. "Feeling better, young 'un?"

"I'm all right," she replied automatically.

"That's good. Much better for you than going 'ome. 'Ave some more o' this. Do you good."

He filled her glass with the cheap Graves, and she gulped it almost defiantly, finishing it. He filled it again, and again she gulped. They were large glasses, and she told herself that she was beginning to feel a bit bosky. But it didn't matter.

Half-an-hour passed in drinking and talking. Then the comic man did a song which no manager could allow him to do on the halls. It went well. They called for more. He gave some impromptus to which Lilac

170

vamped. The company agreed loudly that he was A Lad. Finding her glass empty, Twinkletoes helped herself to more wine. The comic man was certainly comic. And that conductor fellow had wonderfully curly hair. Lilac played the piano beautifully. The Blue Lantern was a jolly fine place. This room was very comfortably furnished.

Roseleaf had settled himself by the electrician's wife, and was stroking her hand.

"Y'know," said the electrician, "I rather feel like a pipe."

"Oh, do yeh?" snapped Roseleaf. "Well you ain't going to git one. Not 'ere, at my party. I ain't going to 'ave you coming up buggy t'morrer, and fusing the plucky wires. You don't take it frequent enough to take it decently. What d'you say, Hilda?"

"Roseleaf's right," said the electrician's wife. "If 'e's on that sorter strike, 'e needn't think 'e'll sleep wi' me. 'Cos 'e won't. I've 'ad one experience. And one's enough. Moderation in all things, as the

171

mother said when she 'ad 'er first baby."

Twinkletoes suddenly shifted her position. "I'd like a shot, guv'nor," she said dully and thickly.

"Eh?" He looked at her with critical affection. "Well, you're in a bit of a state to-night. Might calm yeh down a bit. Won't do yeh no 'arm, I sh'd think. All right, I'll get it."

He called to Dickery-Dock for the lay-out. Twinkletoes drained her glass and climbed to the pillowed lounge in the corner, where she lay down. The lay-out was brought and the stuff cooked. She took the long stem of the pipe to her teeth, and pulled the curtain half-way across the recess. Its dusk was soon beaded with the blue light of the lamp and the tiny glow of the hop.

It was now half-past one. At the piano Lilac worked hard on waltzes, ballad songs, dance pieces, and all the yellable rubbish of the halls. Roseleaf began to tell stories to the electrician's wife, stories with questionable points to them, which he delivered between great gulps of whisky. His stories reminded the other men of stories, and they progressed from coarse to filthy.

The company was well warmed up. Their voices rose. They talked assertively. They became opulent. They looked masterfully at the bottles and the lounges and the room generally. The amber beers and whiskies caught the light and reflected it as gold. Released suddenly from the fetters and cautions of daily life, the men became bold, with a touch of challenge. Roseleaf pulled Lilac from the piano, and settled her at his side on the lounge. One of the bandsmen took her place and perfunctorily hammered out breathless stuff from the Paris halls.

Twinkletoes, through veiled eyes, saw Lilac reclining against a corner of the lounge, her legs crossed. She saw the conductor getting fresh with the electrician's wife. She saw Roseleaf stretch a hand to the table for his whisky, and take a glass of

173

wine and drain it. She saw Lilac fumble for her glass, and take the nearest, which was Roseleaf's whisky. She saw the gigantic Dickery-Dock sprawling full length on a far bench, taking tankards of his own Old, and she heard him exchanging bedraggled jests with the comedians, and discussing probables for next week's big race. She saw Lilac attempt a Mazurka with Roseleaf, and saw her mad feet become entwined with her partner's and her stocking slip saucily down to her ankle, and heard the Homeric laughter occasioned by the accident.

Then a delicious haze dropped over everything. The crashing notes of the piano came to her faintly like music from distant palace windows, awaking in her many forgotten sweetnesses. Dickery Dock swelled into a grotesque statue. The room reeled, and the cloud of tobacco smoke changed violently from purple to amber, to scarlet, to green, and then to the tint and texture of ivory. It emitted gushes of uproar. The lazy smoke

174

from her own pipe, discharging its foul
sweetness, became a wandering angel. Lilac
seemed to swim from the lounge to mid-air,
floating towards her like some cruelly lovely
comrade of a broken dream. The clink of
bottle against glass, as drinks were poured
and swallowed with the hectic haste of semi-
intoxication, was like children's voices singing silvern songs. Through her limbs
purred a fantastic warmth, and she desired
nothing but that that moment should be
stretched to the end of time. Her sorrow
was assuaged. The most profound affairs
faded into ludicrous triviality. Dad seemed
to be only a vague thought from another
world into which she had lately peeped, and
his trouble remained with her as the troubles
of the people of a cinema play. She remembered her furious grief of the evening,
and wondered why she had so behaved. How
silly it all seemed. It didn't matter, really.
Nothing was worth bothering about. She
must have been a silly.

The green-stockinged legs of Lilac moved and receded. Lilac was a dish of goblin sweetmeats which she could never reach. She wanted to eat her, but though she was so close to her she seemed many miles away.

The spent pipe dropped from her languid fingers and fell with a tiny clatter to the floor. Her eyes closed and she and Lilac flew away together. They were still flying, when a hoarse, thick voice, which seemed to be a sentient substance, stopped them. They crashed against it. The words from the voice were:

"S'pose we bett' move along. Wha's time?"

"Ar pars three!" boomed another voice.

"Well. Besserfrensmuspar."

There were sounds of mild scuffling, and surely that was Lilac's voice.

"Amy! A-mee! Don' go yet. I can't g'ome like this. I'm tied up. Sewn up. Fairly. Sha'n' 'alf cop it 'f I go 'ome like this. Lemme g'ome wi' you. My ol' dad'll

176

flog me 'f I g'ome like this. Lemme come
t'your place. . . . No. 'Mall right. Sha'n'
tummel over. On'y gimme your 'and.
'Mall right. On'y daren' g'ome. 'E'll take
the cane t'me 'f I do. . . . Fin' ol' time, eh?
Don' care a damn. 'Joyed meself top-'ole.
Great night. C'm'on. Lemme get your
arm. 'Sawf'ly good of you. Bes' girl I
know. Qui' a dear. Always like you, Amy.
Deares' girl I ever met. 'Strewth, y'are.
C'm'on."

Then another voice. " 'Ere—what about
that kid, Twinkletoes? She's asleep. 'Ere,
we can' leave 'er 'ere."

A great bull roared: "No. Course yeh
can't. I can' ave 'er 'ere all night. One of
you's got to take 'er 'ome."

"Well, who? Eh? Who?"

Three thousand hands were laid upon
Twinkletoes' body, and she dropped from
swirling clouds to something hard.

"Pick 'er up. Pick 'er up," cried the
goblins. "She's drunk."

She felt herself raised by many arms.

"She's drunk."

"Well, what d'y' expect? Mixing pipe with wine."

Then she received a stinging slap on the cheek. Fumblingly she reached the thought that she had never in her life been slapped as most of her young friends had been. Another fierce slap came to the other cheek, and then others from every side, until her head sang.

"That oughter bring 'er round."

"Rub 'er 'ands, someone!"

Rebellion against the idea of assault, more than the assault itself, did bring her round. She opened her eyes.

"Oh! We're all 'ere, then," she said idiotically, knowing that she had said something brilliant.

She saw the electrician's wife stumble towards her.

"You bett' g'ome," said the lady. "Find yer way 'ome all right?"

178

"She can't go 'ome alone like that," protested Dickery-Dock. "She'll be pinched. And then it'll come back on my 'ouse. I don' want no p'lice court case, I tell yeh."

Roseleaf swung himself from the table against which he was leaning. "I'll see'r 'ome."

Twinkletoes suffered one of those electric moments of sobriety that reach the wholly intoxicated. "Don' wanner g'ome. Can' g'ome. Won' g'ome."

Dickery-Dock, the only sober member of the party, scratched his head. "Well, wodyeh going t'do about it?"

Roseleaf dug painfully and deeply into his thoughts. Inspiration came. "I know. I'll take 'er 'ome. Get there, easy. Leave 'er wi' Missis Nobletts, nex' door. Can' let 'er go like this. Can' let 'er be pinched. I'll fix it. Leave it t'me. Leave everything t'me."

"All ri', guv'nor." Twinkletoes reeled towards him, and clutched his coat. "I'll go

179

'long wi' you. You bin goo' t'me t'night."

Now Lilac, who was following Amy and worrying herself to place her feet properly on the steps, heard this, and turned sharply round and screamed, very shrilly:

"No—no—no, Twinkletoes! You gotter come wi' us. Me and Amy. You come 'ome wi' us."

She staggered horribly towards Twinkietoes. "Wi' us. Me and Amy. We'll see you all ri'." She grasped Twinkletoes' arm.

"G'way," muttered Twinkletoes. "Guv'nor's goin' fix me. Bin good t'me t'night. Feel fine. Don' wanner go wi' you."

"Twinks! Twinks!" Lilac tugged madly at her to force her from Roseleaf. "Twinks, you can't. It ain't right. Not wi' 'im. You don' know. You don' understand. You're too nice. Not wi' 'im. Me and Amy'll see you."

"G'way!"

Lilac screamed: "Oh, Twinks, don't!"

"Shut that fool's mouth," said the

electrician's wife, smacking Lilac smartly across the lips. "Yeh'll 'ave the cops on us, makin' that damn row."

Lilac clapped a hand to her hurt mouth, but swayed again to Twinkletoes.

"Oh, Twinks, you can't. You mustn't. Can't you *see?* Wi' us. Me and Amy. We'll——"

Twinkletoes lifted a sturdy leg and kicked Lilac forcefully on the shin. "Now'll you shut up? C'm'on, guv'nor!"

Lilac collapsed on the lounge, and was seized by the protecting Amy. Twinkletoes and Roseleaf, clinging absurdly, found the steps, climbed to the street, and dropped into the tank of the East End darkness. Over everything had fallen that cold crash of stillness that marks the meeting of night and dawn.

The sharp air of the river affected them. It cleared Twinkletoes of stupor, and made her effervescent and reckless. It muddled Roseleaf: he became maudlin and perplexed.

181

"Lessee. Turn to ri', don' we?"

"Thassit, guv'nor. Keep to the right, and you can' go wrong." She laughed stridently.

"Beh no' make s'much noise," Roseleaf suggested.

"I don' care. I don' care fer nothing. My old Dad's goin' to quod, and I'm 'is kid. I shall be a lag's daughter. Won't I be pop'lar? There goes the lag's kid, they'll say. Won' it be funny? They'll throw things at me, and I'll throw back. Winter sports. 'F I go on at Quayside again, sha'n' 'alf get the bird. . . . An' I thought 'e was such a bloomin' 'ero. Such a saint. Something to live up to. And 'e's going to quod. An' me makin' all that fuss in the dressin'-room 'sev'ning. They mus' 'ave thought I was a blasted fool not to 'ave known. Ain't it damn funny?"

"Roun' to ri'," Roseleaf was murmuring. "Rum thing, y'know. Can' find my street. Useter be 'ere. Useter be jus' 'ere. Can'

182

'ave moved it, surely? No; course they can' 'ave moved it. Swear it useter be 'ere. Less ask someone."

He swayed and clutched at a sand-bin, and dragged Twinkletoes with him. They leaned against it, Twinkletoes laughing, Roseleaf apologizing for the removal or obliteration of his home.

Steps sounded sharply on the pavement opposite. Steps they had heard all round them as they walked, but they placed them as belonging to the Blue Lantern crowd. They looked towards the sound, and under a bleak gas-lamp stood Cissie Lightfoot.

Twinkletoes cried festively at her, "Missie Li-ightfoot!" and made a yodel of it.

Cissie crossed the road. She looked coldly upon them. "You're in a nice state, you two."

"What's it matter?" Twinkletoes demanded, holding the sand-bin with one hand and high-kicking with an agreeable leg.

"A kid like you—sixteen—in short frocks.

Oughter be ashamed of yesself, being like this. Stop that kicking. Put yeh frock down, yeh little beast."

"Missie Li-ightfoot, we're lost. Going 'ome with Roseleaf, and 'e's lost 'is 'ouse. Winter sports 'ave just begun."

"Huh! You're a nice one. Out at this hour, and going 'ome like this. And with 'im. Dirty little cat, you."

"That's all ri'. You ain't my mother."

"Damn good job fer you I'm not. I'd give you a few warmings if I was, and like to 'ave the doing of it too."

"I bet you would. Well, show us where Cochin Gardens are."

"Yerss," Roseleaf added, "show us where Cochin Gardens are."

"Find 'em yesselves, yeh dirty little beasts!"

She stood for a moment, and looked upon them. Her face was in shadow, and nothing could be seen of her expression. But when she swung round and walked away, she gave

184

a deep snort as of one at last getting what had long been her rights.

It was Twinkletoes who at last found Cochin Gardens, and she did not put herself in the hands of dear Mrs. Nobletts next door. She disarranged Roseleaf and dug a key from his pocket, and they went in. Roseleaf stumbled to the back room, and Twinkletoes followed, found matches and lit a lamp. Roseleaf dropped to a shiny sofa, and closed his eyes. A few seconds later he opened them, and saw Twinkletoes, wondrously flushed, standing against the table, giggling. He struggled to conjecture how she came to be there. But she was there, profuse in promises of beauty.

"Come 'ere, kid!" he grunted.

IX

CISSIE LIGHTFOOT did not go to
bed when she got home: she was too
cheerful. She sat in a chair until
six o'clock, when the day's life of the place
began. Then she made a sloppy toilet and
went out. On the Blue Lantern corner she
walked with arranged surprise into Hank
Hogan.

"'Lo," he grunted. "'Bout early, ain't
you?"

"Oh, I was just coming out to find my old
pot. 'E ain't bin 'ome. I s'pose 'e's done
a bunk. You know about Minasi's lay,
doncher? Chuck was in it, so I s'pose 'e'll
be roped in with the rest. . . . 'Orrible
business, ain't it?"

"Ar."

"And 'is kid's goings-on make it worse,
don't they? At a time like this, too, when
'e's in trouble. She might 'ave some decency
about 'er."

"Eh?"

186

"Why, you know. Last night. Dirty little cat."

"Ar." He looked her in the face and lied. "I 'card something about it." He had not heard, and she knew he had not heard. It was her plan to tell him.

"Oh. Filthy games. Last night—or rather 'smorning. At the Lantern, 'ere. I saw 'em chucked out. Four o'clock 'smorning. Copped the brewer, fairly. Went 'ome with Roseleaf, too. 'Im, above all. I tried to get 'er away, but she wouldn't come. Flinging 'erself at 'im, she was. Kissing 'im and wouldn't leave 'im. Said she wanted 'er fun same's other people. Swore at me. I saw 'em go into 'is 'ouse together—and you know what 'e is. Drunk? She could 'ardly stand. You can guess what 'appened in there. I s'pose they're sleepin it orf now. Filthy little wretch. At 'er age, too. She wants a 'ose-pipe on 'er. Or a 'orse-whip. And 'er Dad in all this trouble, too. 'Nough to drive 'im orf 'is 'ead."

187

"Ar," said Hank. "But there y'are."

"Well," she continued, after a brief irresolution, "I'll 'ave a trot round and see if I can find Chuck. I dessay 'e's 'ad the wire, but 'e's such a fool. Like as not 'e'll go and bung 'imself at Territon's 'ead—or bash 'im. S'long."

"Cheero."

Hank stood at his corner as though fixed for the day, until Cissie had disappeared. Then with shuffling but rapid steps he went towards Shantung Place. He rapped sharply on Minasi's door. It was not opened until he rapped again with a curious tattoo. Then Dad appeared unkempt, with braces dolefully suspended from his trousers.

"Oh, it's you. Come in. I thought they'd started for me."

Hank walked in. A scene was coming. Scenes always made him uncomfortable, but humanity and friendship demanded that he should carry this one. In the kitchen Dad had been burning papers and other materials

188

in the fireplace. He turned with a mirthful grin.

"Got 'ny news?" he asked.

"No," said Hank.

"Ah, well, They'll 'ave a 'ell of a job to make a case now. I got rid of everything. They can't fix nothing on us. Course, I suppose they'll pinch us, but that won't matter. We shall just go through the 'earing, and then be discharged, and perhaps 'ave a case fer wrongful arrest. There'll be a scandal, but nothing'll stick, and it won't mean anything to Twinks. She'll never know anything. We shall prove innocence, and she'll only be worried 'cos we was bothered at all. So I'm feeling good 'smorning, I was in a fix last night. Made sure they'd got us fair. As it is, she won't know and won't smell anything. Thank God fer that. Thank God." He hitched his trousers, and the prayer came sincerely from his lips. He had passed twenty-four hours of anguish, but now that the thing he

189

most feared was beyond any possibility of arriving, Twinkletoes would never know. She would still believe in him, and he, for the future, would be able clearly and fairly to live up to her beauty and character. He chortled and chirruped: "Gawd is love—'earts are trumps," he went on. "I'v alwis said so."

Hank stood before him, and, taking his appearance, without his face, he seemed some evil thing of the night spoiling the dawn.

"I'm glad," he said at last absently. "But—I mean—is Twinkletoes 'ere?"

"Yerss. In bed."

"Sure?" Hank's face was illumined.

"Course I'm sure."

"Seen 'er?"

"No. But she's there right enough."

"What time she come in?"

"I d'no. I on'y just got in 'bout an hour ago. I bin fixing things at the Works. But she always comes in at 'ar-pars twelve."

"Well—go up an' see if she's there now."

190

"Whaffor? What's the idea?"

"I can' tell yeh—not yet. Go up and see if she's there."

"Wodyeh getting at? You bin on the hop?"

"Go up an' see if she's there," repeated Hank, as from a lesson-book.

Something in his manner and aspect jarred old Dad. He looked at him. He hitched his trousers.

"Go up an' see if she's there?" he asked.

"Ar."

He turned to the door; halted; turned again; looked at Hank, who was inspecting a colored almanac; then went upstairs.

He came down in some trouble.

"Hank, what's the game? She ain't there."

Hank sought for words, and finally stumbled on them. "Old man—your Twinkletoes—your kid's—gorn wrong."

"Gorn wr—— What th'ell yeh talking about?"

"She's gorn wrong."

"Gorn wrong—how th'ell could she go wrong?"

"Well—'ow do girls go wrong?"

A shadow flashed upon Dad's face. His figure bent in menace. " 'Ank—if it was anyone else I'd lay 'em out fer saying that. And you know it. Out with it—wodyeh mean? Wodyeh know? Whassit yer guffing about?"

"I ain't guffing. Your kid's gorn wrong."

Dad fumbled at his trousers. His glance wandered. He scratched his head. Then he blazed.

"Out with it, yeh blasted fool. Don't stand like a blasted scarecrow. Ain't I 'ad enough trouble? Spit it out. Where d'yeh get that blasted lie?"

"She's gorn wrong. Went to the Lantern last night. Downstairs. The Quayside gang 'ave jags down there oncer twicer week. She went with 'em. They come out

192

at four 'smorning. She was drunk. Mrs. Lightfoot see'er. Drunk. And silly. Went 'ome with Roseleaf. Into 'is 'ouse. 'E lives alone. Know the chap 'e is. Four o'clock 'smorning. Drunk so's she couldn't walk. Mrs. Lightfoot watched 'em in. Tried to get 'er away, but she wouldn't come. Said she didn't care. Said she was out for fun same's all the others. Kissing Roseleaf all the way along. That's all."

Dad listened to this succinct report. His face had turned grey. He had not moved from his pose. " 'Ank," he said at length, "it's a lie, a bloody lie. Twinkletoes? Not likely. 'Er? 'Er touch a thing like Roseleaf. It's someone else. One o' t'other girls Mrs. Lightfoot see."

"No," said Hank sadly. "She was certain. 'Sides, could anyone mistake Twinkles fer anyone else? Eh?"

"It's a lie."

"Steady, ol' man. D'you think I'd bring lies like that round? An' at a time like this.

193

Call me a liar if yeh like, but you know me. I didn't pass it on till I'd asked you a few questions, y'know."

"Can't be, 'Ank. Can't be. She ain't that sort. Clean, straight kid like 'er. She wouldn't do it, 'Ank. She couldn't. Gawd wouldn't let her. She's good. She——"

"She's prob'ly there now, ol' man. Must be. You've bin and looked and she ain't bin 'ome. She didn't go in there till four, and it's on'y six now. And she was drunk then. People do all sorts o' things when they're drunk."

"But she wouldn't a-*got* drunk, 'Ank."

"Ar. You bett' come round wi' me and get 'er. Or I'll go round meself, if yeh like."

"No. I'll come wi' yeh. . . . Oh, it can't be 'er. She ain't never done nothing like this before. She was always the straight one among that bunch of kids."

"Ar. But there's some that 'olds back and 'olds back, and wants to be good, and

194

you'd never think of 'em going orf, and then, all of a sudden, orf they goes—like the rest. That's alwis the way."

"Oh, 'Ank, don't talk that way. Not about 'er. She was——"

"Come on, ol' man."

They went out together, Dad still not believing, but too much befogged by the impending police action to make any serious effort with reason. He had been up all night with Chuck, who, in the absence of Perce, had helped him to dispose of certain things whose existence was best forgotten. Of Perce they had assumed naturally that he had got the wire about the coming raid, and had bolted with no spare time in which to warn them.

At the corner of Cochin Gardens Hank stopped, and Dad became suddenly voluble.

"Come on. I'm going in. I'm going to see. If she's there, and anything's 'appened, I'll get old Roseleaf, and I'll——" He paused. His face was contorted. "No,

195

no, I can't go in. I daren't. I couldn't
bear it. If it 'as been—I couldn't face 'er.
Not to see 'er—Twinkletoes. My li'l girl.
Like that. With 'im, too. No, I can't."

"Oh, buck up, ol' man. Come on in.
'Ave the door down. Get it over with 'im,
an' done with it. See what's going on, 'tany-
rate."

"No. I wouldn't dare. It's too bloody.
Can't be true. She can't be in there. It
ain't even fit to talk about. She can't be in
there." He looked up at the house whose
drawn blinds and shuttered front gave it the
aspect of a menacing creature.

Carts rumbled and early tramcars hummed,
carrying their loads of the day's labor. A
Pacific boat had recently berthed, and the
gestic crew was making loud progress to the
Asiatics' Home. Hoarse cries and the
voices of sirens and hooters and the crash of
implements came from the river. A sun
peered from a grey sky and touched the raw
edges of world and people with a wan gold.

196

All externals seemed a part of this sick drama. The very growl of the traffic seemed to Dad like the roll of the drums of fate and the throb of impending doom; and he thought to himself how rum it was that he should have thought of a rum thing like that at such a time.

He irradiated alternately irresolution and a certain sick determination. "Yerss . . . I must go in. I ought to go in. I better go in. . . . Yerss. No, though, I can't. 'Ank, you go. I'll wait. I'll——"

" 'Alf-a-mo. 'Ere comes Chuck. Look! 'E's seen us."

Chuck Lightfoot was charging along the road towards them. His customary morning spruceness was gone. He was haggard, irritable.

"Ah, there y'are, guv'nor. Anything fresh? Think we're all right?"

"Oh, stow it. That don' matter. There's other things. Awful. That ain't nothing to this."

197

"Wodyeh talking about? Nothing to what?"

"See that 'ouse? That's Roseleaf's 'ouse. Twinkletoes is in there. Bin in all night. Drunk when she went in."

"Eh?"

Hank took up the tale, and gave details and lucidity.

Chuck listened attentively. Strange hues chased each other across his face until they settled in a greyness very terrible.

"I tell the ol' man we ought to go in and see——"

"Look!" snapped Chuck. He pointed to the house.

The door had opened. Twinkletoes appeared. Her face was white and strained. Her clothes had been thrown on. Her cheeks beneath the eyes were blackened with dark lines. Her eyes were weary but lit with an uncomely lustre. Her mouth was slack. There was nothing of Twinkletoes about her. She stood shakily, looking on

198

the empty street and the sick morning.

Very swiftly something came to Dad: some sudden change of idea or purpose which communicated itself to the very lines of his figure. Where a moment ago he had suggested helplessness he carried himself with steadfastness. He gripped Chuck's arm; then cried in a loud voice: "Twinks! My Twinks!"

She turned, and saw the three at the corner. She blinked dazily, but her brain told her that they knew and must be avoided. She saw old Dad spring towards her. One thought alone possessed him: Twinkletoes. Gone was all idea of payment to Roseleaf; gone all doubt or disbelief in his girl; gone all loathing of the idea that she had done wrong. She was here; she would want him. But as he approached she screamed, and darted for the gate. The presence of those men filled her with a sudden terror. She fought at the latch like an imprisoned animal. She was mad with

199

dread, while knowing no reason for it. Only she knew that she must get away and hide.

But the latch stuck, and Dad was upon her. He caught her in his arms, even as she loosened it and turned to fly.

"Oh Twinks, my li'l' Twinks. Oh, God my li'l' kiddie."

·Hank and Chuck crossed to them.

"Lemme go," she snapped, between her teeth, very quietly. "Lemme go. Don't touch me."

"Oh, Twinks, what'd 'e do to yeh?"

"Shut up. Don't. Don't ask me."

"Oh, my dearie. Nev' mind. Were 'ere."

"Oh, go 'way. Lemme go. Leave me alone."

"Oh, Twinks, come 'long 'ome. There— nev' mind. I know all about it. Yer all right now."

But still she struggled. "Oh, what's it matter? It's done, now. I don't wanter see none of you—never again. I'm a beast."

"Oh, Twinks, you ain't. You're my

200

Twinkletoes. Oh, yeh dunno what yer saying. Come 'ome now, there's a dearie."

"Go, 'way. Lemme be. Can't I do what
I like? Can't I go orf the rails same's
everybody else? Eh?"

With a savage wrench she tore herself
free. Chuck grabbed at her flying frock,
but the tucks came out with a rip, and she
escaped. Next moment the tortured little
frame fled down the street and turned into
the chain of courts that led from Cochin
Gardens.

Dad looked idiotic and forlorn. He leaned
against the railings of Roseleaf's house,
puffing. He turned to Chuck and Hank.
His hands fumbled.

"She don't want us," he said, looking in
the direction she had taken. "She don't
seem to want us."

Chuck stood staring fixedly at the house.

X

DAD wandered away, and reached Shantung Place with Chuck without knowing how he got there. He went from room to room, but found no Twinkletoes; nothing to flood the day with silver and make work a sacrament and not a mere function.

Foolishly he looked under beds and in cupboards, and in the tiny space of back yard.

Then he stood in the kitchen like a somnambulist, his thoughts dancing a rag-time.

"They'll be 'ere in a minute, I s'pose," he said to Chuck.

"Brace up, guv'nor. The game's on'y just beginning. You'll want yer strength." He was strangely unmoved by the catastrophe. "We've 'ad the wire. That means somebody's giving us a chance. Territon, perhaps; 'e's alwis bin matey wi' me. You're all right. They can't fix us if we're careful. And you got to be careful. It's your job.

For 'er sake. You 'adn't ought to throw up like this. You got to play up to 'er, y'know. You'll want yer strength."

"No, I sha'n't," said Dad weakly.

"Wodyeh mean?"

"I sha'n't. There ain't no need for it now."

"Grr. You'll 'ave to. For 'er."

"No. She don't want me now. And as fer playin' up . . . well . . ." He looked round for something to occupy his eyes. "And it's all come to this. After everything. All I done. All these struggles. Risks and things. All no good. All gorn fer nothing. All smashed. Smashed to bits. 'Er dancing. This little 'ome of ours. That there work-basket I bought for 'er. That Chinese teapot what she bought. And the piano. All fer nothing."

"Oh, brace up, guv'nor. 'Ave a drink and face it out. Can't you understand they're giving us a chance!"

"Yerss. And yesterday I meant to take it. But now . . . All our struggles, just for this. Her ruined. Me in quod. Done for—both of us. And where is she now? Why don't she come 'ome? She don't want me. She on'y wants 'er fling. You could see it in 'er face when she come outer that 'ouse."

"Perhaps she's ashamed," suggested Chuck, in a religious tone.

"Yerss; and good cause to be." Dad suddenly swerved from self-pity to indignation. "Me thinking 'er so pure, so—so different from the other Quayside lot. And me living up to 'er. Tried to. And all the time—— Oh, don't it make yeh laugh?"

He broke down across the table in a wail. "My li'l' gel. Twinkletoes. Pure. And good. I useter take 'er tea and fags every morning in bed. We was so 'appy. We was just like sweet'earts. Living with 'er in the 'ouse, she seemed to make everything good. 'Cos I was a bloody fool and couldn't see what wasn't under me nose. . . . If I only knew where she bolted to. If she'd on'y come 'ome we might fix something. But she don't want me. She's sick of 'er old Dad. Wants 'er fling. She's gorn fair wrong—fer good, I 'spect. Oh! Oh!"

"Look 'ere, ol' man. I know 'ow our worry at the Works started. Y'know my old cow and me don't get on—about Twinkletoes. Well, y'know that day I give a 'iding to Perce? Well, I went for 'im 'cos 'e touched Twinkletoes. My ol' woman got 'old of 'im, found out why I did it, found out 'e wanted to get back on me, and put 'im wise to fixing us. Showed 'im 'ow to give the whole caboodle away, and then levant. Met 'er 'smorning—laughing mad, she was—and she told me. It was 'er way of getting back on me, 'cos of—'cos of——"

"Huh!" said Dad, barely interested. "I thought there was something behind Perce's staying away. So that's it. So it all comes back to Twinkletoes. Oh, God Almighty."

Chuck lit a cigarette. "That's why we got to fight it out. It started from 'er, and

205

it's our job to stop it—for 'er sake. Well, guv'nor, 'ow 'bout it? Going to take a chance?"

"Oh, don't. Cancher see it don't matter? I don' care a damn. Don't matter what 'appens now. We're done. We're out. 'Er ruined. Ruin and disgrace. Everybody'll know it. All over the place. Can't never 'old up our 'eads again. But don't you stop. You take yer chance."

"I'm going to," said Chuck, with apparent callousness. "So long, guv'nor. It can't be 'elped. These things 'appen every day to someone, and now it's our turn. We got to stick it. It's our luck. So long."

"So long, boy."

Chuck left by the back entrance.

Dad stood by the kitchen table, rigid, for a length of time, until a double knock came at the door. He opened it to Divisional Detective-Inspector Territon.

"Ah, Minasi. Bin looking fer you. There's some trouble about your place, and

I got to make a few inquiries. In the mean-
time——" He entered, closed the door, took
some official papers from his pocket, and read
from them in a sing-song, detached voice.

"That's all right," said Dad. "I'm ready.
It's quite all right. You don't need to bother
with no inquiry. I bin on that lay now for
four or five years—reg'lar."

"It is my duty to warn you that——"

"That's all right. I know all about it.
It's quite true. I must a-bin a silly."

"Well, you better get your hat and coat."

"Righto."

"You look pretty bad."

"That don' matter."

He threw on hat and coat, and he and
Territon went down the street together,
Territon chatting amiably about the weather.

.   .   .   .

At midday Cissie Lightfoot arranged herself for an excursion. She washed. She
dressed with some attention her honey-
colored hair, scented it and curled it. She

207

chose a mercerised cotton blouse which began its business as clothing some minutes too late. She also chose appropriate stockings and shoes, bought from the tally-man.

She took a westward bus, and left it at the corner of Commercial Street. She walked down the street, and was then in the Russian quarter, the most melancholy of all London slums.

Reaching Brick Lane, she turned, and thereafter made many turns until she rested at a door in a cruel, brooding passage. She knocked. The door was opened by a hairy Russian.

"Perce?" she asked.

The Russian inspected her and drew back the door. She entered, and without further talk went up a steep, fusty stair and knocked at a door on a tiny landing. Perce appeared.

" 'Lo," he said vacantly.

She pushed her way in and looked round the room. It was dim and fusty, without a carpet. It contained a low, fusty bed, table, chair and samovar. On the table was a glass smelling of vodka. On the chair rested a lamp and a little tin, but no pipe.

She sat down on the bed.

"Well, I fixed you all right, ain't I?"

"Well, I ain't 'eard anything so far."

"No more you won't. You won't be worried. Territon was too anxious to get what I could give 'im. I tied 'im up proper. 'E 'adn't got nothing to go on when 'e got the office from the—you know—the place where I started it. I give 'im what 'e wanted on one condition."

"Ah?"

"And that was—you."

"Good."

"Um. And I fixed everything with 'im, without telling 'im anything 'bout you. You're as safe as 'ouses now. You can come back if yeh like, on'y you'd better run straight fer a bit. They won't touch you, old son. Territon's a damn fool, but 'e's straight. When 'e's give 'is word 'e keeps it."

"Good. Good. You bin a good pal to me."

"Yerss, I 'ave. And I got a name, too."

"Sorry, Cissie. Yerss, you done me proud."

She leaned back on the bed, her eyes half closed.

"Well!" she snapped suddenly.

"Eh?"

"Ain't there more ways'n one of saying thank you."

"Why . . . Well . . ."

"Oh, shut up!"

"Why, now, I——"

"Perce, now . . ."

"Oh, well, I——" He grew awkward, hot, inarticulate. He stood by the small stove, looking in all directions. There was a minute's silence.

"Perce," she said at last, "I ain't told you everything. Come here—there's something else. Come here—'case anyone's listening."

He went to her.

210

"Sit down."

He sat down.

"Perce," she said, in a voice intentionally weak and intimate, "Chuck's bin such a beast t'me."

"So?"

"Yerss."

"I'm sorry."

"Ain't I bin a good pal to you?"

"Course you 'ave."

"Well, then. You've paid your one on Chuck, without any risk and you couldn't a-done it without me. And you ain't said you're glad yet. Not prop'ly."

"Oh, well, I am. Reely I am."

He got up and walked to the window. The woman shut her hands and glared. She thought deeply and coldly.

"So that's 'ow yeh treat yer friends, eh?"

"Why, now; no. 'Tain't that . . . but . . . I mean . . . You don't understand."

"Grr. I understand right enough. Sooner you're with the rest of 'em the better, I

211

reckon. I s'pose you're after that Minasi
kid—eh? Well, she ain't for things like you.
I will say this about the others. Although
they make fools of themselves over her, they
were straight about 'er. They did take care
of 'er. You know that from when you started
messing about with 'er. But you, yeh little
snipe, I know what you're after."

"Now, look 'ere. 'Tain't that at all. You
don't understand."

"Understand yer grandmother!"

He turned from the window. Clearly he
was in a nasty hole.

"Oh, well."

"Oh no," she retorted airily, rising from
the bed. "I don't want that kind of payment.
I don't want to 'ave to ask for thanks. If
you ain't got the sense or the decency to be
grateful when anyone does you a good turn
—why, then, you can—you can go to 'ell,"
she shouted. "Straight away. And none too
soon neither." She marched to the door.

"No; but 'ere——"

"Oh, go and boil yesself. And eat it after-wards."

The door slammed.

Perce slouched about the room, hot and, as he put it, fair flummoxed. He had no conscience; it had been stifled by the pipe fumes; but he hated to hear himself and his tendencies described so fluently. How could anyone get interested in an old thing like Cissie? A great sprawling thing like that. And without any sort of what d'ye call it. But she'd got him. Got him fair. It was fair sickening. He looked again at the lamp and the tin, and regretted that he had left Limehouse in such a hurry that he had for-gotten his pipe. He didn't know anybody in Stepney who had a pipe, or any place nearer than Limehouse where he could get one. She had said he could go back. But that was before the rumpus. He wondered if it was still safe. Whether she would blow the gaff on him at once, or whether he'd have time to nip down to a certain shop in Chinatown, and

213

get a pipe, and nip away to a certain friend in Notting Dale who might afford him sanctuary.

Then his thoughts became practical. The sensible thing to do was to levant at once for Notting Dale. She was in a wax, and she'd surely do it on him at the first available moment. He oughtn't to waste a moment. But the imagined fumes of chandoo floated about his face, and all thoughts of safety sped away. He wanted a smoke. He must have a smoke. He looked longingly at the lamp and the tin. Bliss was there; only a pipe was lacking. Was it worth risking? Foolish hesitation. One smoke was worth any amount of chances. Besides, even if she did peach on him, perhaps they wouldn't be able to prove anything. After all, he'd passed the information. He might turn King's evidence. But supposing he did get jugged. Prison was a horrible place. Why couldn't he make up his mind at once? If he only had a pipe he could think clearly

214

after a smoke and know exactly what was
the best thing to do and how to do it. He
ought to have a pipe, because then he would
have no trouble in planning a get-away;
the best place to go to, how long to stay
there, and how to fix things with the Notting
Dale bloke.

Pipe won.

He took a long overcoat and a blue scarf
and cap, and went forth to the east. He
bought a pipe, and was striding along to the
tramcar trembling with anticipation when a
bulky figure stopped him.

"Perce Moxon. Want a word with you,"
said the figure with terrifying amiability.

Perce started like a rabbit, meditated
flight, but found his legs unwilling to serve
him. He looked up and saw the sonorous per-
sonality of Divisional Detective-Inspector
Territon standing between him and peace.

"Let's go somewhere where it's quiet, so's
we can talk, shall we?" said Divisional Detective-Inspector Territon pleasantly.

He linked a friendly arm in Perce's, and took him across the road, while the lad mumbled obscene oaths to himself, the pipe protruding from his armpit like a derisive tongue.

XI

AFTER leaving Shantung Place by the back entrance Chuck Lightfoot did not go home. He went to the house of a boxing friend with whom he sometimes stayed after a markedly heavy quarrel with Cissie.

There he washed his face and took fresh clothes. He dressed hastily, carelessly. He looked with surprise upon his familiar collar and tie and boots. It seemed queer that these commonplace things should have passed with him through such sickening happenings without change. The very sight of them aroused hatred; putting them on for the last time in such circumstances, he could not forget how he had arrayed himself in them in pleasant days.

At eleven o'clock he went out, coming, by shy alleys, to the Quayside. He went unchallenged through the front of the house, and, passing through a heavy door, reached the back. He climbed to Roseleaf's office.

217

Roseleaf was standing before a mirror in which he caught the picture made by Chuck in the doorway. He turned.

" 'Ullo," he said, with the fatigued affability of the music hall manager. "What you doing 'ere? Who let you in?"

"Walked in."

"Oh. Well, what's yer business—or yer good news?"

"None. Just dropped in to pass the time o' day and what-not. . . . You 'ad a bit of a night last night at the Lantern, didn't you?"

"A night?" Roseleaf chortled, and then stroked his head with a suggestion of great suffering. "Don't ask me. Talk about a night! Don't know whether this is Piccadilly Circus or Good Friday."

"That's an old one," said Chuck. "You got that from Willie Wangler. But I 'eard about the night. By the way, what 'appened to young Twinkletoes—Monica Minasi. She 'ad a good oiling, didn't she? Went 'ome wi' you, I 'eard."

"Ah, she did. Couldn't shake 'er orf. Never knew I was so fascinating."

"Um. 'Er old Dad can't find 'er nowhere."

"No? Well, don' ask me. She come 'ome wi' me, but when I woke up 'bout eight o'clock 'smorning, she was gorn. I dunno what 'appened. I was too boxed. We all were. Fair canned. Up to the Plimsoll mark. What a night? And what a little red wagon that kid is. 'Strewth!"

"I believe yeh," said Chuck appreciatively. He entered pleasantly into the spirit of The Night. " 'Er old Dad see 'er come from your place, but she done a bunk soon's she saw 'im."

"Aha! Didn't want to be caught on the naughty-naughty, eh?"

"That's about it." He leant casually against the doorway, smiling and chuckling in response to Roseleaf, who rattled on at his whimsical confessions. "Must a-bin a night. Sorry I missed it."

219

"You'll have to come along another night," said the genial adventurer. "What a furnace! I shall never remember all what 'appened after we left the Lantern together—nor won't no one else. Never saw a crowd so binged as we were. If you got a 'ead like what I got this morning you'd be raving mad. I got some kind o' faint recollection that when we got indoors we—aha!"

"Aha!" echoed Chuck. "I bet you did. Trust you. And then?"

"Ah, no. No telling tales. I won't give it away. Never give anyone away yet. No one can't ever say that o' me. . . . I feel I ought t'ave enjoyed myself, and I s'pose I did; but 'tain't no good enjoying yesself if yeh can't remember it, is it? I wonder what she feels like 'smorning. Pretty rotten, I guess, what with one thing and another. Well, we only live once, and I say——"

He stopped. He had his back to Chuck, and was standing at the mirror arranging his elaborate lilac-sprigged neck-tie. Through

220

the mirror he saw that Chuck had taken four quick steps, and now stood behind him. In his hand he held a life-preserver. It was raised.

Markie Roseleaf was jerked from his overnight stupor with a cold shock. The shock brought a certain streak of sense to him. Sense sufficient to stimulate quick thought; sufficient to realize the imminence of attack; sufficient to know that he must act at once; sufficient to plan four ways of putting Chuck fair and square on the floor. But though his brain moved rapidly, it was moving without control from him; he could do nothing. Through the mirror he saw the preserver descend.

Markie Roseleaf dropped in an untidy heap before his mirror. He heard Chuck say:

"Die—you! Die! Fer Twinkletoes!"

Three times the preserver descended, and Markie Roseleaf died ere his lips had finished mumbling: " *'Ere—stop it now.*"

Chuck wiped the preserver with the inside of his coat, and stuffed it in his trousers pocket. Then he went out, carefully closing and locking the door behind him. He returned to the house where he had made his toilet.

.   .   .   .

Cissie Lightfoot was white with rage as she walked from Stepney to Poplar. When she reached home she opened a bottle of beer and ruminated, while swallowing sobs of mortification. That filthy little Perce to turn her down! She had not only done him a tremendous service; she had paid him the compliment of going to his rooms; and he had given her the frozen face. However, she had settled with him: a few words to Territon had dragged his particular pride to dust.

It seemed that things were not developing at all as she had projected. She had paid Twinkletoes, the principal cause of her domestic distress; and she had paid Chuck

222

and others of the gang who had worshipped
the kid. But where did she come in? She
had looked to receive as well as pay. She
had overlooked the fact that disposing of
certain troublesome people would have the
effect of leaving her very lonely; and it was
only when she realized this that she made
her random cast at Perce, who should have
provided solace, lacking anything better.
Now that he had thrown her down she was
left stranded, and she began to cast about
her for some possible pickings.

From the muddy bottom of the beer bottle
crawled an idea: Twinkletoes.

Nobody knew of Cissie's part in the game.
She was the stricken wife of a bad man who
had brought disgrace upon her by his secret
misdeeds. That disgrace had fallen on other
people too; there would be quite a lot of
trouble around Poplar. Well, now, how
commendable it would be if the stricken wife
should come forward to soothe a fellow-
sufferer. After the arrest of the gang

Twinkletoes would be left friendless and probably homeless, for since her behavior with Roseleaf no respectable people would take her in. But one of the sorrowing company could do so without arousing neighborly comment other than approval of a praiseworthy action.

Yes, she would do the beautiful thing. She would take Twinkletoes into her home and look after her; and she could explain to any who wondered that, after the trouble she herself had gone through, she had a fellow-feeling for others, and desired, if possible, to rescue Twinkletoes from the evil associations with which she was surrounded, so that the child should have every chance of avoiding such disaster as had fallen on Cissie, and be safe from any temptation of getting into bad hands and going permanently wrong.

The more she rested upon the idea the more closely she cuddled it. The child had never suspected her; had always been friendly; and in the panic that would seize her at the downfall of her little world she would be ready to fly to any arms that promised a haven.

As she thought of that white flake of girlhood, her mind turned into itself and wove intricate patterns from certain amiable dreams which had frequently, though not markedly, visited her. She suffered hectic raptures; scaled secret topless heavens. All Poplar would know by now what kind of child was Twinkletoes. She would let the neighbors know that she intended to bring her up by rigid rules, keep her straight. She would properly guard her, and whatever measures she might find it necessary to employ would be universally tolerated, for all would recognize the need for a firm hand when dealing with such a bad girl. She would be a mother to her, or, in the event of her playing any more wicked games, a stepmother.

She chuckled. She inspected her hands

225

as she pondered—long cold hands and arms
that hung like silver swords. Monstrous
emblems arose in her mind and produced a
condition of agreeable hebetude. She had
cast herself for the part of stepmother, and
it appealed to her; it contained possibilities.
With Twinkletoes on call, tedium would be
pleasantly negatived. Beer and tobacco and
tea were losing their bite on her; this new
distraction promised the filling of many
waste hours of day and night; and she
shivered in a mood of intoxication keener
and sweeter than any that alcohol had given
her. There would henceforth be no need to
keep beer about her; when she wanted
amusement she would have it at hand. She
drifted into reverie, and floated on adumbra-
tions of luxuriant indulgence. With the door
of her ugly room locked, the blinds down,
and the crevices of the windows muffled
. . . she stretched her hands as though
Twinkletoes were already within grasp.
Yes, it was a pleasant idea. She would have

complete license to do as she liked, and there could be no fear of subsequent trouble, for by the time the gang came out of prison she would be in other quarters with Twinkletoes well broken to her will.

Later she began her search for the child. She was sure to be somewhere about. She went at first to the man most likely to know: one Spud Cohen, who, trading as Gaston Leclercq, combined various businesses: that of variety agent, turf commission agent, moneylender, private inquiry agent. Spud Cohen, like Hank Hogan, knew all that happened in the district; it was his business, where it was Hank's pastime. She did not go to Hank; she feared to make too many inquiries in that quarter.

Spud Cohen was at his office—one little room in East India Dock Road. He was greasily dark, and was lazily dressed in soup-splashed clothes. Rings glittered blatantly on his fat fingers, and a cigar rode jauntily on his lips. His features were small, with

227

eyes that seemed to deny their existence.

"I'm looking for a girl," said Cissie.

"So'm I. We all are. All the time. Aha!"

"Yes; but I mean a partic'lar one."

"Who?"

"Minasi's kid—the dancer. Seen 'er?"

"She was trotting around 'ere. Bin trotting round all day, I think. Looking scared like."

"Well, I want to see 'er partic'lar. If any of the boys come across 'er you might get 'em to send 'er along to me at my place. Tell 'er I got something important t'say."

"Righto. By the way, Chuck's mixed up in this Minasi business, ain't he?"

"Yerss."

"Bin copped yet?"

"I dunno. Ain't seen 'im since 'smorning, and then 'e on'y swore at me and marched on. I 'spect they got 'im by now, though."

"Mm. Nasty business fer you. Sorry."

"Thanks. Can't be 'elped. Don't forget about that kid."

"Righto. I'll send 'er along if we come across 'er."

At four o'clock Cissie heard a knock at the door, and when she opened it a pale, beaten figure crawled into her menacing room. All buoyance was gone from her step, all laughter from her face, all tranquillity from her heart. Her legs that had danced so many glad legends to Poplar people lagged. Her arms hung like withered flowers. She had been across the river all day at Rotherhithe, wandering and dreaming and brooding. The stupor from the previous night had been blown away, and her mind and body were now clear—clear to accept all the misery that had been hurled upon them. If only she had known, it wouldn't have been so bad. If they had told her, if she had been aware all along of her old Dad's game, she would not have minded. She would have loved him as deeply, and his little aberrations from honestly would not have troubled her, for she had a great capacity for smiling on sin

229

and roguery. It was the deceit and trickery
that so hurt her. She had been brought up
to regard theft and forgery not as wicked
things, but as things which pleasant people
didn't do. She had been brought up to
regard her Dad as a straight man; he had
carefully nourished that illusion; and all
the time he had been a bad man. If only
he had let her into his secret, she would have
supported him cheerfully. But to think
that he and Chuck and Hank Hogan and
the Pearly Prince and Dick the Duke and
Wallopy had all been in this conspiracy to do
dirty things and keep all knowledge of their
ways from her, and leave her to find it out
after the whole world knew. . . .

If she had known, she would still have
admired him, still have kept herself straight,
still have been happy. Instead, she had been
kept in the dark, and now that light had come
to her from alien skies it had dazzled and
bemused her.

The first realization of her position came

in the yellow evening when a far-away organ gurgled one of her dance tunes, a lonely melody shot with the sadness of happy things enchained; and she discovered a longing for somewhere to rest, for some face that she knew, some familiar background.

People recognized her in the street, and pitied her, but passed without the customary greeting, kindly or flippant. Trouble was coming to the Minasi group, they had heard, and when they saw her they passed to the other side or disappeared into shops. It was none of their business. You see, you could never tell. You might easy get mixed up in a thing like that, and have to go to court as a witness, and have your name printed in the papers, and everything; and look at the disgrace and the exhibition you made of yourself then.

Thoughts of her companions came to her, but she felt that she could not face Dad, even if he were free and she could find him, and she didn't want Lilac or Wallopy or the

231

Pearly Prince. There remained Chuck, and it was to Chuck that she instinctively turned. As his name came to her, she suffered a gnawing hunger for his stolid presence; he would understand. So she returned immediately to Limehouse, through the Rotherhithe Tunnel, and at its mouth she met a lad who gave her Mrs Lightfoot's message. At once she sped to the Lightfoot home, connecting Chuck with the message and thinking to find him there.

"I 'eard you 'ad something to tell me," she said, as she stood before the smiling Cissie.

"Yes, dear. Sit down. I was wondering about you. What you going to do now?"

"Oh, I dunno. Where's Chuck? Ain't 'e 'ere?"

"No. I dunno where 'e is. I ain't seen 'im all day. I expect 'e's copped, same's as your father."

"Dad copped?"

"Um."

"Oh! Oh, lemme find Chuck!"

232

"Well, now, never mind Chuck. You're in trouble, dearie, and I don't know what'll become of you, things being as they are. So I thought I'd better find you and look after you. You won't be able to keep that 'ouse up, and you'll probably get the sack from the Quayside over last night. You was silly not to come away from 'im when I told you. However, it's done now. So I'm——"

But Twinkletoes was not listening. She stood limply, with a distant expression on her face.

"I want Chuck," she said stupidly.

"I tell you 'e ain't 'ere. You're going to stop with me now, and I'll see that you don't get into any further mischief. You'll be all right with me, dearie." She looked fondly at the child, and found herself all-of-a-trembling at the limitless prospect before her. The forlorn, helpless figure set her pulses leaping as though some strange beast were inside her.

"No, I want Chuck. I want to talk to
233

Chuck. Ain't 'e coming back 'ere soon?"

"No, I tell yeh. Come 'ere to me, child."

"I must find Chuck. I must."

"No, you mustn't. You're not going out again to-day, me lady. If no one else won't look after yeh, I will. And later on you'll thank me. You'll thank me for taking care of yeh. You're going to be my little girl now, and now I've got you 'ere you'll stay 'ere. You bad girl. If you think you're going off gallivanting again to-night, you're wrong. Just because yer Dad's gorn, don't think yeh can do what yeh like. Them that's older'n you will 'ave to look after you and stop you from doing dirty tricks that'll lead you to don't know what. My 'usband worked fer your Dad, so the least I can do is to look after the boss' kid."

"Oh, don't. I want Chuck."

"It's all through yer Dad's spoiling you that yeh've gorn wrong. I'm going to make it my business to see that yeh don't go wrong again. See, child? And when you've got

234

over this nasty mood you'll thank me. See?
No nonsense, now. What you want Chuck
for? Always 'anging round my 'usband you
are, yeh nasty girl. I believe you got something on with 'im, yeh dirty thing! You're
not going out again. Best place fer you is
bed. Go on. Get into the bedroom, and
don't let me 'ear another word from yeh."

"No. I got to see Chuck."

She turned away. Cissie darted forward.
"Stop 'ere—you. Don't you dare——"

But Twinkletoes had turned the handle.
Cissie stretched a long arm and grabbed one
of the drooping curls. With a swift movement Twinkletoes turned and struck the
hand away, and scuttered down the stairs.
Cissie rushed to the landing. "Come back
—you. Come back. Stop 'er, someone.
You——" Then: "Gorn. Damn and blast
'er. After Chuck, too, the little cat. Nev'
mind. I'll get 'er to-morrow. I'll get
Territon on to 'er, and get 'em to detain 'er.
And when I do get 'er . . ."

235

XII

WHEN Chuck returned to his temporary lodging after settling his account with Markie Roseleaf he fell into a chair before an empty grate and wandered in a night of thought. He thought of his first meeting with Twinkletoes: how the loveliness of her had swept into his dusty soul and cleared it of many foul spots; how, though he had sunk into a pool of drink, his mind, through his squalid defiance of life, had been sweeter and cleaner than it was when he had accepted life and lived straightly. It seemed strange that this should be so; but he was no philosopher, and he let it pass. He thought of his commonplace marriage, and the terrible woman who was Mrs. Lightfoot. He thought of his early athletic days when nothing worried him; when he knew nothing of beauty or of love, and was content. He thought of the storms that Twinkletoes had brought into his placid career.

Since he had known her he had seen his life and its surrounding from a detached point, and all had seemed dirty. All his possessions became mean. Limehouse was dirty. Boxing was a dirty game. The Blue Lantern was dirty. Beer-drinking was dirty. His wife and his home were dirty. His early disregard of the dirt had been dirty. His habits and speech were squalid. There was nowhere any touch of the decencies, the finer lights of existence. He felt that all folk must despise him as he despised himself. All those things which were not part of the glory of Twinkletoes he loathed. At sight of her he would become precipitately abject: a thing of no account. Everything pertaining to him was without wholesomeness and dirty; so dirty, he felt, that, however he labored, he should never fully cleanse it. Wherefore he let it go, contented himself with loving Twinkletoes and refreshing his soul, while his animal self added dirt to dirt through the doors of the Blue Lantern.

But that was all over. He was through. At last his hell had burnt itself out, and he was free of further torments. He sat, unable to move, for many hours, until the wide afternoon shrank imperceptibly into scrupulous dusk, and snow began dejectedly to fall.

It fell upon a slinking, pursued little figure that crept towards this house, her black frock fluttering against the whitened street like a great moth. At the house she hesitated; then moved to the window which stood flush with the street. The blind was up, and, as she peered, she saw, and gave a half-strangled gasp of relief at the slack form of Chuck, head on chest, stretched in a chair. She tapped the window. He looked up swiftly. "Oh, Chuck, Chuck, I want you," she whispered to herself.

He stood for a moment blinking at the window and the round, peering face that filled it, as a man might at some improbable ghost.

Then he opened the door, and she tottered

238

in, her little shoulders powdered with snow, her throat and young breast wet with it. She tottered in and fell to the low chair.

"Oh, Chuck, Chuck!"

"Twinkles! Oh, my dear. My sweet!" was all he found to say.

He went to her, and knelt before her, and she clung to him as to the only tangible, steadfast thing in a world of shadows. Arms locked, breast to breast, they lay until the dark came, and the frail, heaving body found rest. Then she talked stupidly, as people talk whose sensibilities are in suspended animation.

"Oh, Chuck, why's all this 'appened? Why's it all come like this? Dad a swindler. Me gorn wrong. You a swindler. Prince and Duke and Wallopy—all swindlers. All going to prison. Oh, why wasn't I told about it? Going on all this time. And I trusted Dad and everybody so. I thought they was all good. Seems like everybody's bad."

Chuck crouched in silence. There was no defence.

239

"Twinks," he said at last, "it's funny.
. . . We've all bin bad 'un's, and all this
'as 'appened 'cos of you."

"Me?"

"Um. Your Dad wasn't bad. 'E done
what 'e done 'cos of you. 'E done it just to
get enough money to give you a chance, and
then 'e meant to drop it. 'E 'ated doing it.
And 'e wouldn't do lots o' things 'e might
'ave done that'd bring in a lot o' money.
Just enough to get you started—that was
all 'e wanted. And 'e worshipped you so.
Like me.

"Twinks, I ain't got much time left.
They'll be after me, soon. But you know,
sweet'eart, 'ow I've loved you, don't you?
I 'ave. Love you like I never loved anything
before. You'll never know what you was to
me. You're so young and I'm older, but I
loved only you. Nobody's ever loved me.
All my life I've wanted to be wanted. Chaps
are like that, reely, more'n girls. When I
first see you, there was something—some-
240

thing—I dunno. I knew nothing'd be the same afterwards. I knew you was part of my life then."

She moaned and leaned towards him, but took his declaration of love without foolish wonderment. Subconsciously she had known his feelings about her. He took her fragile form again into his arms, and kissed her cold cheek and her lips, murmuring: "O lovely, my lovely!" Lips locked to lips they lay in the austere intoxication of first love; and even while his mind cried at what he felt to be sacrilege, he showered kisses upon her face and neck. It didn't matter. It was the last time. The end was near. Something enormous and supernally beautiful came to him in those embraces. He became transfigured. He discovered some new strength in himself; some revealed significance in common things and the squalid story of which he was a part.

"Twinkles, my lovely. That's the first and last time I shall ever kiss you. Funny—but it seems like there's something behind all this.

241

Something kind of big—better than us. It's all round everything; sort of as if you'd found something you'd bin looking for a long time and then forgotten. You—so lovely and good—and then all the trouble, and—and everything. And if you, dear, 'adn't been so lovely and good it wouldn't never 'ave 'appened. I wouldn't a-done what started it."

"What started it?"

"Um. Me going fer young Perce—that was what started it. When 'e messed you about that day. I thrashed 'im."

"Oh, Chuck."

"Your Dad was just throwing up the crooked business, and nobody'd ever 'ave 'eard anything about it if we'd stopped then. But my missus got 'old of Perce. She knew I loved you and she 'ated you and me 'cos of it. So she got back on both of us by putting Perce up to giving us away, knowing 'e owed me a grudge fer that thrashing."

"Oh, what's the matter with me that I've

242

brought all this on ev'body? And you, Chuck—I was alwis fond of you. You was so splendid and strong and kind. What did you go in for the dirty work for?"

"I din' go in fer it until after yer Dad 'ad started it, and I met you. I was driv to it, Twinks. By you. It was 'ell 'cos I loved you, and you wouldn't never be anything to me, and my missus gave me 'ell too 'cos I got fed up on 'er. I couldn't face things after I met you. Nothing seemed good 'cept you."

"Oh, me—good!" she said ironically.

"So I went on the drink, and then got in with your Dad's business. It was all that was left."

"It seems such a muddle, don't it, Chuck? And I never knew nothing. Me doing all this. And all I wanted to do was to make ev'body 'appy."

"Yerss, I know. But there y'are. Things go their own way; and you can't help 'em."

She broke down in a little tempest of sobs. "People used to love me so, and say I was

243

pretty and make 'em feel good, and all I do is to bring rottenness everywhere. All this 'cos I made people love me. Oh, Chuck, do you remember our afternoons in the Works when we was so 'appy?"

"Yes, dear, I remember. But I wasn't 'appy. I was miserable, reely, but——"

"I'm sorry. More sorry now. . . . And do you remember the night at the party when Wallopy made that speech about me—and the things I said? I never thought what was coming. Silly fool—I thought everything was going on always like that. Then, do you remember that night I come to see you fight at Battling's Ring—and you gave me one of your gloves after the fight? I've got it still—at home—in my drawer. And how I told you, first time I met you—that I'd be your sweetheart. I didn't understand then, Chuck. I do now. I know such a lot now, Chuck."

"Oh, my dear, I remember. All of it. But don't talk about it. It'll only hurt you

244

worse. I ain't told you all yet, Twinks. Your Dad was arrested to-day. He could 'ave made a clear case and got off. Somebody was giving us a chance. They couldn't 'ave proved much against 'im. But when 'e 'eard what 'appened to you, 'e didn't seem to care like. Lost all interest. Waited for 'em, and when they came 'e confessed. I 'eard about it. Twinks, m'I ask you a question?"

"Um."

He hesitated, searching for delicate words and finding none. "Twinks—what made you go to the Lantern last night and go wrong with Roseleaf?"

"Oh, I dunno. I was mad. Everybody knew about Dad, and when I got to the theatre all the girls chipped me and ragged me. And when I found it was true I didn't care what I did. Nothing seemed to matter then. If 'e'd gorn wrong there was nothing for me to keep straight for. Then I got mad and didn't care what I did. Dad was a forger, and never let me know. Deceiving me like that."

"Yes; but, Twinks, don' be 'ard on 'im. 'E didn't like doing it and 'e done it all fer you."

"Um. That's what's so awful about it. Everybody who loved me seems to 'ave copped out. All through me. Me—Monica Minasi—a kid."

"There's still something else you got to 'ear, Twinks. You won't never see me again. I sha'n't never come out o' prison."

"Chuck—no, no!"

"Yes. Y'know Roseleaf?"

"Um."

"I went round and killed 'im 'smorning."

She gave a short scream, and her eyes held terror. "Killed?" she whispered. "Killed?"

"Yes. 'Cos of what 'e done to you last night."

She sagged from his arms and lay limp, staring upon him with stricken eyes and dropped mouth. The tortures of the last

246

twenty-four hours had deadened her senses, and it was some time before this fresh blow brought with it fresh pain.

She pressed her hands to her ears. "Oh! Oh! Me—again? And you'll be——"

"Yes. I felt like killing my missus too. It started with 'er. But I didn't. I'll let 'er live it out."

"Oh! Oh! You murdered someone?" She suddenly thrust out her legs, and screamed silly screams and laughed. "Forging. Murdering. Getting drunk. Going like a street girl. Aha! So this is what loving people means. Is it like this with ev'body? And we was so 'appy." There came a swift revulsion of feeling. She flung herself forward and upon Chuck, screaming: "Save me! Save me! Oh, Chuck—save me. Me and you. Save yourself. You can't be—— Oh, save me! I'm so frightened!" She flung impassioned arms about him.

He grew delirious and babbled foolish words. "Oh, my little love, my little sweet-

'eart. Oh, I can't. I can't do nothing for yeh. My little bird. O lovely girl. O little princess, I can't 'elp you."

She pushed him away and tumbled in a heap to the chair, wailing and crooning and making noises terrible to hear.

"Oh, what's to become of me? Oh, Jesus, save me. I ain't done nothing to deserve all this. I'm on'y a kid. I ain't got nowhere to go now. Mrs. Lightfoot 'ates me. I'm ruined. Disgraced forever. I ain't got no friends to go to. Oh, God, God."

"Twinkles, Twinkles. Don't. You 'urt me so. It ain't no good. It's all 'appened like this. 'Tain't nobody's fault."

She lay back and panted, and after a while grew calmer.

Presently she spoke: "Chuck—get me a drop o' water."

He went to the back of the house for the water. When he returned with it she was gone.

He set it on the mantleshelf and looked

248

at the black grate and then at the chair where she had sat.

"Ah, well," he said. "Ah, well," and flung the water into the fireplace.

Later he went out and called at the Blue Lantern.

"Pint o' the Old, Dickery."

He looked at the pint of the Old, and remembered how often he had looked at similar pints in this bar; and he fumbled with the thought that this would be the last time he would look at a pint. He thought of all the commonplace acts of his daily day, and they became alive with interest and strangely lovely. He thought of his morning walk to the Works, and the people he met as he passed down the street. He thought of his bus rides to the west, and the elaborate bars where he met the successful boys who placed the spurious notes manufactured by Minasi. He remembered how the morning sunshine fell on the streets, on St. Paul's Cathedral, on Temple Bar, on the

249

Gaiety Theatre, and he remembered these places as the most beautiful of all landmarks. He thought of his beer and bread-and-cheese at eleven o'clock; of his cup of tea at the Works with Twinkletoes; of the sociable evenings with the boys; of his Sunday jaunts to the Forest; of his morning shave; of his Saturday night bath; and the painfully romantic Saturday evenings when he watched Twinkletoes dancing at the Quay-side; and he could have wept for the hidden charm of these things suddenly revealed to his parting glance. They sped through his mind in the brief moment between stretching his hand to the tankard and grabbing it and drinking largely. Then, as the stuff assuaged the scorching of his throat, he was instantly cold and calm.

Hank Hogan was in his corner, suppressing, at great strain, the news of the day.

" 'Lo, Chuck. 'Eard about it?"

"What?"

" 'Bout Roseleaf."

"Yes, I 'eard about it. Found dead, wasn't 'e?"

"Ar. Smashed to pieces. Rotten business last day or two, ain't it?"

"Yes; ev'body's copping the knock."

"Ar. They got the Dook and the Prince and Wallopy to-day. Minasi give 'imself up, too." He lowered his voice. "They ain't got you yet. Can they pinch you on it, or are you fixed?"

"Oh no. They'll 'ave me when they like."

"Ar. Wonder who done Roseleaf in?"

"I wonder."

Hank looked closely at him. Chuck met the glance.

" 'E cert'ny asked for it," said Hank.

" 'E did. An' 'e got it."

"Ar."

Again they exchanged glances. Then Hank looked away and became silent. There was never a man like Hank for minding his own business at the right moment. Chuck finished his pint and moved to the door.

"Well, so long, old 'un."

"So long, lad." Then, as an afterthought: "Goo' luck."

"Thanks."

Chuck turned into the main road and proceeded to a blue lamp some two hundred yards away. He walked into the station and went to the sergeant at the desk.

"I done a murder."

"Didn't quite catch."

"I done a murder."

"Where?"

"Markie Roseleaf, manager of the Quayside. In 'is room. Bashed 'is 'ead in. I done it with this."

He planked the preserver on the desk.

"Yes. Consider yourself detained, pending inquiries."

.   .   .   .

It was a night of storm. A shrill sky screamed of sleet. Great gales rushed from the river, annoying loose windows. Shop signs swung grotesquely and complained in

252

creaking voices. Skirts and coats were flung
and buffeted, and hats flew and lamplights
flickered. Nothing that was not heavy or
made fast was allowed to stand. The wind
took everything broadside on, with full, considered hammer strokes, or in swift swirls,
darting in with a hundred light blows from
this side and that. Ropes in the Docks
whistled. Cranes jerked and jangled.
Brown sails bellied and slapped themselves
with determined glee.

The river, of the hue of molten steel,
heaved and rushed angrily, slucking against
staples and barges, or rising in ineffectual
splashes to the low-lying wharves.

The little waves and spears of water
seemed, to the girl who had reached a wharf
by climbing from the bridge to the Isle of
Dogs, to be so many arms stretched in
invitation. Before her stretched the yellow-
starred length of water; behind her was a
lofty street of houses, at the expansive midnight loud with humanity, now, at ten o'clock

feebly lit, reticent, forbidding. Aided by the gale, noises flowed from mid-stream with fluid ease.

Twinkletoes, her lemon-colored curls streaming from her head in a furious bid for flight, stood with her tiny hands outstretched against the wooden supports. She had come there to ask why. And sometimes she choked with incipient sobs and sometimes she moaned her thoughts.

This was the end. Her god—her old Dad —the maker of her character—had fallen. All her beauty, her high character, her gladly nourished ideals, gone to dust; and in the going carried disaster to those she most loved. Now, at the moment, she was learning the lesson that we may place our trust in nothing but our own souls; for, when all our faith rests upon one idol, and the idol falls, it falls upon the faithful heart.

No more would her romantic legs twinkle for the delight of Poplar, or her expressive arms gather in their thousand woes. No more would her baby body flit about the streets scattering smiles of carnival and goodfellowship. No more would folk wait to hear her light feet chattering to the asphalt pavements, to see her break the dusk with colored frock and daring ribbons hanging about her like petals of a flower, the whisk of them kissing the little stockinged knees. No more would the gallery boys cry: "Are we to part like this, Bill?" In vain would they shout: "We—want—Twinkletoes!"

Perhaps an hour later her question was answered.

Perhaps she knew why all that is sweet and clean and true must ever be bruised and broken to make easier the jungle of life for the cruel and the faithless. Perhaps she knew why beauty and character must be held at such a hideous price. Perhaps those tiny hands that had so often supplicated to bunches of violets did not supplicate in vain for an understanding of all the weeping that had been brought upon her little kingdom. Perhaps those tiny hands that had so often soothed the querulous or caressed the lovable gathered elsewhere some share of balm for her throbbing wounds. Perhaps that lovely little heart, wracked with more tortures than it was ever made to bear, found a kind resting-place enduring when the radiant limbs and happy body were no more.

.   .   .   .

In the four-ale bar of the Blue Lantern Hank Hogan lounged in his corner, and Dickery-Dock attended him.

"Difference it's made, ain't it?" said Dickery.

"Ar."

"If anyone'd told me all this would 'ave 'appened in about a week—all at once, as you might say—I'd a-called 'im a liar. Wouldn't you?"

"Ar."

"Chuck gorn.   The Dook and the Prince collared.   Minasi waiting fer trial.   Perce

lagged. And li'l' Twinkletoes disappeared.
. . . Sickening, ain't it?"

Hank Hogan looked through the open
door to the evening life of the Lantern
corner. The cars were still running. The
Lascars were still jungle-treading. The
golden boys and girls were still "clicking."
The straight form of Division-Inspector
Territon still moved from point to point.
He himself was still drinking beer. But the
goodly company who made the Blue Lantern
worth while . . .

"Yerss," he said, "nothing don't seem the
same. Fair sickening. But there y'are.
That's alwis the way."

At the window of her cottage sat Cissie
Lightfoot, her vindicative fingers gripping
a tarnished Bouquet novelette. She was
smiling, intent on some sociable thought, her
dull eyes lit by a secret flame. She too
looked upon the soft evening, but the absence
of certain characters was by no means fair
sickening to her. She looked upon the

257

parading girls, moving with the demure, steadfast carriage of adolescence. The imperious urge of youth raced under their translucent skin. They were awake for love, and soon Tunnel Gardens would be delicately noisy with laughter of those caressing and being caressed.

As she looked upon their sylph-like forms she thought of many things, and the thoughts seemed to satisfy. She thought of Twinkletoes, who had been just such a one: asking for it and getting it where it hurt most. She thought of Chuck, and decided that she had done well. He had told her to lay an egg, and she had laid it, and had made him look silly, as she had threatened. She had asserted herself, and made him realize her. She thought of Old Dad in his cell, awaiting the Central Assizes, and of Roseleaf.

"Serve 'em all right," she thought. "They asked for it. Damn clever they were, but what's it brought 'em? After all their games what's it brought 'em?"

To her it had brought only loneliness, almost intolerable loneliness. So that each night when the dusk came and blotted out the processional street she would drop the blind, and loosen her hair—now of a bilious hue—and take a black bottle from its hiding-place, and stretch herself on the bed.

THE END